THE COLONY
AND THE
CAVEMEN

DEWEY M. ERLWEIN

Wasteland Press
Shelbyville, KY USA
www.wastelandpress.net

The Colony And The Cavemen
by Dewey M. Erlwein

Copyright © 2006 Dewey M. Erlwein
ALL RIGHTS RESERVED

ISBN13: 978-1-60047-074-5
ISBN 10: 1-60047-074-2
First Printing – February 2007
Cover art by Graham L. Spahn

Printed in the U.S.A.

ACKNOWLEGMENT

I wish to make known my deep appreciation for the countless hours my wife Marilyn spent guiding and editing this story. Also thanks go to my daughter Maxine who took time from her Masters studies to read and interject writing wisdom and mentoring whenever I needed or asked.

I am also grateful for many who encouraged this effort, including Helen, a high school classmate, who helped proofread and edit.

Cover art and illustrations are done by Graham L. Spahn

INTRODUCTION

Fraya finally got her wish to fly to another planet. She was a rising star in the ranks of scientists at Centre, the government's space agency, but left after false charges were filed against her by a jealous superior. She had the good fortune to be recognized as a genius by Arin Restor, an industrialist. Restor wanted to sponsor the first manned landing on Terres, the neighboring planet, and sell artifacts for profit. He contracted Fraya and her boyfriend Rami to manage a commercial program that sent a crew of three space-pilots to Terres to make the first manned landing. The trip was so successful, the artifacts made enough profit for the commercial venture to finance a second follow-on trip.

Rami, an environmentalist, feared global warming on Baeta was leading to a fresh water shortage and the eventual end of civilization. He proposed that Arin sponsor colonization on the new planet as a way to preserve the species. Arin was only interested in profit and notoriety, but agreed a colony on Terres might discover future valuable resources. He sponsored a second trip. Rami and Fraya selected a group to fly with them to Terres as a potential colony. While on the ground on Terres, their control building back on Baeta was destroyed, and they became stranded. Rami made friendly contact with the natives (Neanderthals) and the colonists learned to survive off the land.

Earth was inhabited by two-legged vertebrates we know as Neanderthals. This story has Venus a hypothetical wet planet, populated with technically advanced upright bipedal creatures, two hundred thousand years ago. In this story, Venus, number two, is called Baeta, and Earth, number three, is Terres. The two planets are similar in size, but there the likeness ends. Earth rotates clockwise three hundred and sixty times each year. In contrast, Venus rotates only once, and backward, resulting in approximately a half year of light, and a half year of darkness. Rapid cycles of day and night as we know them does not occur on Venus. The settlers from Baeta had to adapt to a completely new, different diurnal cycle, on Terres.

This is the fictional story of the second manned space flight from the number two planet to the number three planet, intended as a round trip. Technical problems stranded the travelers on Terres, and this is the story of their survival and propagation.

TIME AND DISTANCE:

Venus rotates backward compared to the rest of the planets, and slowly, about once each year. A complete rotation is called an annur. For purposes of time and measurement, Venus is divided into 100, wedge-like arcs; each arc (of rotation) takes 2.43 Earth days, or 58 Earth hours, and 100 arcs equals an annur. A milliarc is 3.5 Earth minutes.

For distance perspective, a quant is about an arm's length; 1000 quants, a kiloquant, and is about a half mile.

1. THE LAUNCH

In frigid blackness, vapors issuing from joints in the frost-covered fueling lines looked like fuzzy spears in the flood lights. The main tanks were being topped with cryogenic liquid fuels and Fraya shivered at the groaning noises from the expanding and contracting metals. Like fingernails on dry glass the piercing sound made her teeth ache. She knew the temperature outside was near freezing and was grateful for the warmth of the pressure suit.

"Rami those noises seem awfully loud, don't they? Seem louder than they should be?"

Rami looked at Fraya and saw the concern on her face. He smiled. "They sound louder because we're actually inside the ship instead of watching from the control building. It sounds like ripping metal from here, but it isn't."

"I hope it doesn't make the passengers uneasy." She stared at the monitor, mesmerized by the images formed by the illuminated mist. One coupling was leaking more than the rest.

"Look! Rami ... a stream of fuel is squirting from one coupling then arcing down to the pad in slow motion and bursting. The floodlights make it look like an explosion of curious vipers with hooded heads snaking about the pad and then rearing up.

"Very pretty but I've never seen a coupling leak like that before. Have you?"

"No. I hope its all right.

"Are you all right Fraya? You've seen many launches before."

"I'm really just tired. I'm sure everything's fine." Suddenly, her face blanched. "Rami!"

He turned to the monitor in time to see the coupling spilt apart and the hose become disconnected. Liquid fuel started spraying out of

1

the open end and an automatic slam took place. Activated by a pressure drop in the line, a solenoid closed a valve to stop the flow. Rami watched helplessly as the vapors dissipated, concerned that a spark might cause an explosion. Everything seemed to happen in laggard motion; the liquid falling to the ground, then splashing to vapor and then evaporating. He stared at the monitor; watched the fuel-flow stop, then let out a sigh of relief when the vapors appeared to be mostly gone .

Fraya looked to him for a clue as to see how serious the situation was.

"We get at least one malfunction on every launch Fraya. I hope that was ours for this launch."

"I hope so too Rami." Her focus returned to the flickering monitor.

The picture roiled and wavered each time the sequencer automatically flipped up a different image and Fraya blinked hard trying to clear her vision. It was frustrating for her because the visor covered her face and she couldn't touch her eyes. Also the breathing mixture flowing into her helmet had the unpleasant odor of old hoses and made her eyes water further distorting her vision.

She wiggled and tugged at some of the loose wrinkles in her suit. "This suit doesn't fit me very well Rami. Who ordered it?"

"I did Fraya. I'm sorry. They only made two sizes and neither fits you. I know it's pretty bad but we'll be in zero gravity before long and it'll be over soon Fraya. After we launch, then you can rub your eyes all you want. Besides your eyes are not the problem: It's a bad picture."

The standard pressure suit was heavy fabric complete with a hard, dome-like helmet and except during a short training session she had never been in a complete spacesuit before. She felt smothered

2

and swallowed a strong urge to rip her visor open in order to draw a deep breath.

The passengers watched the screen with Fraya and Rami, listened to the countdown and waited. Corky, the commander had activated the speakers in the dimly lit cabin so the passengers could hear the dialogue between pilots and controllers. An electronic voice snapped the count following a ... tic ... tic ... tic ... that seemed to be in sync with some of the instrument lights above the pilots; rows of lights on the overhead panels that rolled in glowing patterns of yellow, green and red.

"What's the holdup?" Corky asked. "We could have boiled a basket of eggs by now, one at a time."

Fraya recognized the controller's voice; a controller she had trained and assigned to handle this launch.

"The board is mostly green Corky," the controller said. "All reds are gone; two yellows yet, but nothing serious. Programs are finished transferring to the intelligencers and fueling is complete: It won't be long now."

"What about the disconnect in the fueling line? Did we get enough fuel before it broke?" Corky asked. Corky Kraejil was the flight's commander and one of the pilots Fraya had hired away from Centre and into the commercial space venture. Fraya was one of twenty rookie space-travelers strapped into web seats behind the three pilots, listening to the countdown and watching the views on the grainy monitor.

"We were lucky on that one Corky. Fueling was almost done and no sparks occurred. Let's get you off the pad before any other opportunities for your problem-solving skills show up."

"It was just routine Cubic, but that really was enough excitement for one launch. We are ready to go," Corky replied.

"Good." The controller paused very briefly. "The last hold has just been cleared Corky, and the countdown has been resumed. Ignition sequence is about to start."

"Glad to hear that," he replied. "The passengers are getting anxious."

The serenity of the pilots had a reassuring effect on Fraya. As she watched them she finally started breathing easier. If any of the three pilots had serious anxieties they hid it well. Corky Kraejil, the commander, was a veteran of many space flights and had an ego that defied description. If Corky felt anxiety he wouldn't let on even if he was about to explode. He was always a picture of composure.

The other two space-pilots were seasoned veterans and seemed almost as relaxed as Corky, calmly sitting and waiting for the launch. During the countdown a controller's voice periodically broke the silence requesting the pilots cross-check an instrument with one in *Cubic*. Cubic was their nickname for the command, communication, and control facility. At one point Fraya saw Kel's head bob and she thought he was dozing, but when he reached out to touch an instrument or adjust a setting she realized he was just very relaxed. Kel was the shortened name for Mikel, the second-in-command. Kel would occasionally point to a log being held by third-pilot Caleb and nod at one of his entries.

This was the second manned space flight to Terres. The first, four annurs earlier, had three pilots aboard, and no passengers. Kel was one of the pilots. Corky had been commander on that flight, as he was on this flight, but Caleb was new to the program. Caleb was an experienced Centre space-pilot that Corky had recruited to replace Glennick after Glennick's accident.

Corky and Glennick had gone down to the surface on the first trip while Kel stayed aloft on the Barge. The two had gone on an exploratory hike and were on their way back to the ascent vehicle when the accident occurred.   Glennick was hit by a rock thrown from above by a hostile Terreling and was knocked unconscious. Corky carried him back to the launch vehicle, got him aboard, and up to the Barge. The three left the Barge and started the return flight back to Baeta but Glennick never regained consciousness.

The electronic voice sounded again resuming the final countdown with abrasive Klaxons burping around the launch area. Speakers blared the last few counts; ... five ... four ... three ... : Cerebel, the command module, began to shiver: The monitor showed umbilical lines disconnecting and dropping away from the rocket, and gantry arms swinging away from the assembly with mechanical creaks, clanks and bangs.

"Vibrations here," Corky told the controller.

"That's good Commander, because you're lit and starting to fly."

Flames poured from the nozzles of the three auxiliary rocket engines strapped to the sides of the Dynamo-One, searing the launching pad, and briefly blinding the imagers turning the screen white. The rocket assembly swayed slightly then began its vertical ascent trailing a cloud of flame and smoke with acceleration forces that kept the crew and twenty rookies glued back against the webbing in their seats. Fraya slid her hands to the edges of her lap and cupped her abdomen.

The calm composure of the pilots had assured Fraya, but just at ignition, she felt a little spasm in her belly that took her attention away from the monitor and left her briefly startled and gasping. She put her hands over the site of the spasm and, as much as she could through the pressure suit, pressed lightly on the spot. She swallowed her concern.

"Terres here we come!" Corky grunted in a stiff voice distorted from the strain of acceleration. "I hope my wallet is in the Barge. It's been missing since the last trip and I think I left it there."

As the big rocket carrying the passengers sped away from the launch pad and the space ship gained speed, Fraya felt her face stretch from the acceleration forces. She imagined her cheeks were being pulled back toward her ears and felt like her arms had weights around the cuffs. She kept her hands around her belly and quelled a wave of nausea. She meant to do a self test for pregnancy before launch, but was afraid of the result, and afraid if she had told Surg about her suspicion, he would have scrubbed her from the flight. So she kept her suspicion a secret. She was determined to go to Terres and all her work, plans and objectives were culminating in this flight. Besides, she had reviewed the data from flight tests performed at Centre on pregnant animals in space and became convinced that if she was pregnant, the trip would be very low risk to either mother or child. She and Rami had worked for annurs to make this venture a reality, and she wasn't about to forfeit her seat unless she thought harm may come to her or the baby. She stole a glance at Rami and saw he was locked onto the monitor. *This is going to be one incredible adventure,* she thought.

2. LOCAL ORBIT

Fraya was finally getting her flight into space: Not just a simple orbital flight but an interplanetary trip with the possibility of standing on the soil of another planet and looking back at Baeta, the planet she called home.

This flight had been one of her coveted objectives since childhood when she used to stare up at the twinkling sky through hand-held magnifiers to pick out the planets. Before she completed mid-elementary tutelage she could name and identify every planet in the solar system and most of their satellites.

Lift-off: The instruments and lights in front of the pilots looked like a kaleidoscope of color and activity. They were riding atop a big, throbbing Dynamo rocket engine with three burning solid-propellant boosters attached to its sides. When the solids burned out and peeled away acceleration slowed slightly but the change was hardly felt by Fraya. She didn't feel much change until the big Dynamo completely stopped its burn. Then the sudden lack of thrust threw her forward against her harness.

"Main engine shutdown," Corky announced.

"Took your foot off the accelerator, did you Corky?" the controller asked.

"That's affirmative and everything's green so far."

We're following you here also Corky," a controller in Cubic announced, "and agree the flight looks normal so far."

Corky looked at a monitor showing a view behind them. "The big dynamo is loose and we can see it drifting behind us. I'm lighting up little Dynamo now."

"Let me know when its lit corky. I'll give you a thrust reading after you throttle up."

"It's lit and Dynamo-One just disappeared below us as we sped away. Dynamo-Two may be smaller but it sure has a big kick."

"Thrust coming up now nearing ninety percent. You will be at orbital velocity in three milliarcs."

Fraya was just beginning to feel the sensation of free-fall when the smaller Dynamo kicked in. The thrust slammed her and the others back into their seats with a push that remained steady until the craft arced over to parallel the surface at orbital velocity and then Corky shut down the second engine.   They were back into free-fall.   The passengers were mostly silent; just listening to the exchange of communications. There was little to say except to grunt or comment about the sensations of the launch and now, the sudden absence of gravity. They were coasting around their home planet. Corky saved fuel in Dynamo-Two for later maneuvering.

Dynamo-Two was dormant and quiet, and the craft was now in silent orbit where the rate of fall matches the curvature of the planet. Fraya gulped at the sudden shutdown and grabbed at her shoulder straps.

"Rami, we're falling?"

"Technically we are, Fraya. You physicists call it micro-gravity, but you know what's happening ... it's free fall over the horizon."

"I know and I'm sorry for the outburst.   But even though expecting it, I wasn't ready." She calmed a little and let her arms float out in front of her. The sudden quiet made conversation deafening and Fraya reduced the volume in her headset and lowered her voice. A few small objects began floating around in the cabin.

"It feels like a dropping elevator Rami."

"Good analogy," he said. "We'll adjust soon, I hope."

"At least the suit isn't chafing me now." She felt the twitch in her abdomen again; fleeting, but it began to worry her a little.

Silently coasting in orbit, darkness changed to light for thirteen milliarcs and back again, as they passed into and out of the planet's shadow.   The sunlight temporarily boosted Fraya's mood and she concentrated on the monitor.

On-board scanners showed the view below, but Ardena and their launch area were still in darkness. In the sunlight, Fraya could pick out the eastern end of Scorpia and Bacamir and wondered if Centre technicians were watching them on their radar. *Probably*, she thought. She could see the north side of Scorpia and picked out Montes and the peak of the Great Mons, the highest mountain on the planet. The peak was usually cloud covered but this time it was clear and she got a quick glimpse on the monitor. The planet's curvature was visible and a slim, blue line of atmosphere that seemed thinly out of proportion appeared under space blackness.

"The views are spectacular, aren't they Rami."

"Yes Fraya. So far the views are making up for the disappointment we felt when we couldn't go on that first trip."

"Actually, not being on that first trip turned out to be beneficial. That trip was a rehearsal for this voyage and answered a lot of questions about landing on Terres," she said. "And of course having the Barge there, proven and waiting for us in orbit is a big plus."

"And the four annurs gave us a chance to really get organized, select good candidates for the trip, and do some training. It was a long wait but we're on our way now."

"Not quite Rami. I guess I considered this project just a job and not getting my hopes too high until we actually lifted off the pad. We still aren't on our way until we get out of orbit here and start the crossing to Terres. Then, and only then, I'll say we're on our way."

"When that coupling broke," Rami said, "I thought it was over; that the whole thing would explode. I held my breath until the vapors cleared."

Fraya nodded. "I did too, but I'm feeling pretty optimistic right now."

Ardena was midway through its half-annur dark period, a season that frequently depressed Fraya, and when their orbiting craft coasted out of the shadow into sunlight, she felt as euphoric as a child on a swing. The depression was swept away from her head and giddiness engulfed her, at least for the thirteen milliarcs until they reached darkness again.

"Am I grinning Rami?"

"Yes Fraya: Obvious even through your face plate.."

As the experienced space-pilots predicted, most annoyances of the pressure suit did go away in the weightless environment but another discomfort took its place. Fraya began to feel nauseated. By the time they entered the second orbit she could think of little else but the queasiness, and wondered if the spasm was related to the nausea. She tried hard to concentrate on the monitor views below as they passed through sunlight, but the effort helped very little. She knew she was going to vomit, and wondered; was it the weightlessness, or possibly a pregnancy. She felt too ill to really care which one it was.

"Kel, I'm going to throw up."

Assigned to coach the passengers, Kel unbuckled his harness, floated up in front of the group, and turned around to face them.

"It can happen to anyone. You'll be fine in a short time Fraya. Open your visor and use the bag in the seat pocket." He floated over to her and helped open her visor just in time to put the bag over her face. The vomit projected into the bag and he showed her how to zip it closed before any of the material floated back out.

"I'm so embarrassed," Fraya said. Kel assured her nausea was common even among space-pilots. One of the others reacted to the sight of her retching.

"Kel, I'm also feeling sick. What do I do?"

He grinned. "It'll pass. If you have to, throw up into that little bag in the seat pocket. Caleb has some anti-nausea medication and will pass it around. Let's all take one of these tablets to prevent any further problems.

"I'll need water to swallow this Caleb," said one of the recipients.

"Coming right up." Caleb propelled himself over to a stowage bin and grabbed a plastic bag with a stoppered spout. He opened it and demonstrated squeezing to eject a stream of water into his mouth. "Don't squeeze too hard and try to catch all the water you eject." He passed the container around. Before long all the rookies had opened their face-plates, taking sips of water and awaiting the next instructions.

Kel kept moving around the group, chatting, encouraging them. "We'll keep orbiting until our Cerebel catches up with the Annex, people. Two or three more orbits should do so hang in there. Corky will be maneuvering until we match the orbit of the Annex and then he'll close the gap. Each maneuver requires a small burn, which sounds like a bang or pop, but don't be alarmed. It's a good noise and means things are working. Meanwhile you'll stay in your harnesses until after hookup.

Fraya's nausea had not passed as quickly as she hoped. Even though ill, she tried to maintain some poise and set a good example as leader of the group, not only for Rami, but for the others. It was difficult to look dignified while vomiting, she told herself, but she couldn't suppress it. By the time they entered the third orbit she was feeling better and let her mind drift.

"People." Corky broke the spell. "We've caught up with the Annex. We'll connect shortly. I'll need Kel and Caleb up front in the command module for awhile."

The craft consisted of three parts; the command module, the annex or living quarters, and the propulsion unit on the back end of the assembly.

11

"After we dock," Kel informed the passengers, "Caleb and I will go into the Annex, connect all the cables and hoses, and make a systems test. Then if all is well, we'll let you un-strap and practice moving around a bit. You will be able to float up and peek into the Annex, but then we'll get back into our seats in Cerebel where we'll all stay until we boost out of this orbit and get on with the crossing to Terres.

The only sound they heard for a while was the hiss of steering thrusters, and a pop each time a short maneuvering burn took place. Corky slid the nose of Cerebel into the capture ring on Annex and finally, the clank of metal against metal and a shudder throughout the structure let everyone know they had made contact. Locking rings pinged and Corky exhaled a loud sigh that could be heard over the intercom when the spring-loaded latches engaged on the first try. He accentuated the sigh with a blast on a horn, and an announcement.

"We're in, people: hooked to the Annex."

3. FRAYA'S START AT CENTRE

Even though the prestigious Centre was in a foreign territory Fraya decided at a young age she was going to work there. Centre was the only organization on the planet capable of launching objects into space and if she was going to be a part of the celestial studies she had to go to Centre. She knew it may be the only opportunity she might ever have for working on space programs. It easily won her imagination.

Centre scientists had sent a number of probes into the solar system getting images of the rings around number six, the red spot on number five, the reddish tinge of number four, and the white clouds on number three. They had also built and assembled an orbiting space laboratory they called the platform. The pieces were built in a factory, launched individually and assembled in space while in orbit.

Fraya's main celestial interest was our own solar system and more specifically planet number three.   After she completed her graduate studies in Bacamir and achieved the top credential in academics, she was accepted as a scienomie at Centre. She was initially assigned to a Research department and in a short time had invented a new molecular gyro system subsequently used on all flights. She became a favored prodigy and was considered by many to be the future head of all trajectory and space navigation projects to be launched from Centre.

Alas, a jealous superior interfered with her future. Prior to sending a manned mission to Terres, Centre wanted to explore some of the surface with unmanned robots. Program scientists first built and sent a simple spacecraft, called Alpha-Surf, to orbit the planet, sample the atmosphere, and radar map the surface. Following that they sent two un-manned robotic probes called Settlers to land on Terres. The first one slowed and began to orbit around Terres then strangely disappeared on the back side.   What happened to it remained a mystery.   Hirl Lockni, the project manager, tried to rationalize the disappearance by saying it was probably hit by a meteorite. Many on the governing council accepted his explanations and the investigation was closed, but some of his technicians thought his commands to maneuver Settler-One were errant and it probably entered the atmosphere at a wrong, steep angle and burned.

Fraya quickly concluded that Lockni was charming, glib, and persuasive, but technically incompetent.   He had made several impulsive changes to trajectories for previous robotic flights and the mistakes were not highlighted. The blunders were inconsequential, did not cause catastrophic failures, and were generally corrected in time by

13

competent technicians. The mistakes were generally ignored and only the successes were highlighted.

The most notable project so far had been the Terres orbiter, Alpha-Surf. When Alpha-Surf made it into Terres orbit and began mapping the surface, Lockni was lauded by his superiors for the achievement and given an unchallenged mandate to manage the Settler project. However, the technical differences between dropping a spacecraft into an orbit around a planet and actually getting it out of orbit and successfully settled onto the surface are immense. The orbit is just step one in the landing process.

Most of the council members responsible for funding the Centre programs were charmed by Lockni's presentations and readily followed his explanations of possible failure modes for Settler-One. His theory of a possible meteorite strike was accepted with few questions.

The second robotic craft, Settler-Two, once went out of control while underway, and left the planned flight path. The transponder signal was lost and Lockni, fearing for his reputation, did not want a second failure on his record. He already knew about Fraya's brilliance and asked her to correct the trajectory and get the craft back on course.

"You know, of course, that I am assigned to the research department and would have to work for you on a loan basis."

"Of course," he said, "and you know that given time there are many skillful members of my crew that could recover this robot, but we need action now. Your reputation for developing non-linear quantum orbital-mechanics is so impressive I would like you to chair the recovery operation and be discreet about it. My crew will be in awe just to have you in the group. I assure you they will cooperate with you to get the Settler back on track."

Fraya was actually eager to accept the assignment but did not want to seem overly zealous. In the recesses of her thoughts she saw an opportunity to be assigned to the Terres Project and that was her primary interest and goal when she started at Centre anyway.

"And I will see to it the loan assignment is approved and you will be free to work with my crew."

"One other condition," she said, "I really want to be assigned to work on the Terres Project."

"Why, how perceptive you are;" Lockni smiled, almost bowing, voice syrupy. "I have a transfer authorization all filled out ready to make you a permanent member of this project as fast as possible."

"I'm sure we can salvage the craft, but I do have a question. What did you mean when you said be discreet?"

"It's not really important but I thought it would cause less concern among the councilors; who fund these programs by the way; if the anomaly was minimized. So I suggest, if the question comes up, you can say the craft went a little off course; but was never in danger; if you know what I mean."

"I'll do the job and I'll answer any questions honestly if the subject even comes up."

"Fraya that sounds very professional to me. I would expect nothing less, and I thank you."

4. COMPELLED TO LEAVE

Fraya willingly joined Lockni's crew in the control room, established a rapport with the lead, and coached him to do some corrective maneuvering. Subsequently the craft stopped its tumbling, straightened, and got back on track. Transponder signals were re-acquired and the craft continued on its prescribed course. Settler-Two made a successful intercept with Terres, orbited into its solar path, and settled to a soft robotic landing.

Settler sent back enough images from the surface to show that life forms did exist on Terres but its transmissions failed soon after the landing. Before it failed, the controllers saw vegetation, and the imager automatically captured a view of an upright bipedal humanoid. Lockni never saw that picture. It was hidden in the imager's memory and nothing was showing on the screen. He privately wished Fraya had been available to diagnose Settler's malfunction and try to fix it, but he had already sent her away on a new assignment as part of his scheme to get her out of Centre. She thought she might be rewarded with a position on the Terres project after rescuing the robotic lander from its erratic flight but it didn't work in her favor. Her actions saved the flight of Settler but word leaked out that she had been responsible for the rescue and some of the council members began to doubt Lockni's competence. Lockni's jealousy escalated. Even though he had requested her help word of her participation made the rescue a bitter victory for him.

As he promised Lockni had Fraya assigned to the Terres project and then promptly maneuvered her into an assignment developing a new space engine. His motive was getting her away from Centre and the Terres project. She found the new assignment interesting and challenging, but it took her away for long periods of time. She traveled to many different subcontractors and found one in her home territory of Ardena, near her parents' home, that had promising technology . Prollett had been utilizing a nuclear reactor for superheating water to break-down temperatures and ionizing it into a combustible fuel. It became known as the *nuper*.

While Fraya was coordinating with the Prollett people to perfect the nuper, Arin attempted to hire her into his newly formed commercial space company but she declined, saying her loyalty remained with Centre. Lockni's undercover agents made covert recordings of her conversations with Restor and then claimed she was disloyal and treasonous. He had her arrested in Bacamir on false charges of disloyalty. Lockni alleged she was giving away technology to Prollett and pushed for incarceration.

Fraya was tried by a magistrate but acquitted and seemingly free to go. However, Arin Restor reasoned she was still in danger from Lockni so arranged to have her secretly hidden in Bacamir until she could be smuggled out. He started a new company for commercial space business, covertly brought her back to Ardena, and hired her to manage the operation.

Fraya was very depressed, knowing she could no longer work at Centre, but Arin's offer to manage a commercial space venture gave her a new chance to continue her creativity but at Solport, working for Arin, instead of at Centre. She accepted the offer.

5. THE COMMERCIAL PROJECT

When Settler-Two was settled on the Terres surface, powered up and activated, it revealed some vegetation, briefly saw a humanoid and then suddenly quit transmitting, as if it had been damaged. The controllers back at Centre received nothing except a carrier signal. Lockni had no explanation for this failure, but thought he could eventually blame it on Fraya.

Arin Restor, the subcontractor making the nuper engines, had a desire to get into the commercial space business but not for mere communications satellites; he wanted to be the first to land a man on Terres. He envisioned not only global prestige but enormous profits from the artifacts that could be brought back.

17

Fraya talked with him about the goal of a manned landing on Terres and she recognized it as an opportunity to personally go on the space flight she dreamed about. She convinced her boyfriend Ramizia Wog to join her. With Arin's backing and business knowledge Fraya and Rami built a factory, made some nuclear-thermal-propulsion engines, a staging craft to remain in orbit around Terres and an interplanetary spaceship to fly to Terres, land and return.

Among the pilots who rotated assignments on the Centre platform was Corky Kraejil, a leading candidate to eventually fly Centre's manned trip to Terres. Ironically about the time Fraya began thinking about a flight crew Corky became available because of a misunderstanding between him and the flight director. Centre had a cadre of pilots that rotated assignments on the orbiting laboratory and flew special test missions. Corky was high on the roster as the leading test pilot, but when a crew list was posted for the eventual manned trip to Terres his name had been crossed out by the Director. The director accused Corky of having an affair with his pledgemate and he scratched Corky from the crew list. Corky denied the allegations then resigned from Centre in disgust. Then he called Fraya.

"Corky did you seduce the director's pledgemate?" Fraya asked.

"Are you kidding? She's a lush and came on to me. I sure don't need a pledged woman with so many unpledged women available and willing. Besides the claim of me and his pledgemate is simply not true."

"All right, come to work for me. I need you."

* * * *

18

Millen was Fraya's closest friend at Centre. He was Centre's *mission planning specialist* and frequently took meal breaks with Fraya. They exchanged the latest gossip and he kept her posted on Centre's politics. She also suspected he had a crush on her and she always felt comfortable around him because he never made implicating remarks or comments. When she asked him to leave Centre and join her on the commercial project, he eagerly accepted. He was bored with his work, and the challenge of a new project sounded too exciting to miss.

Millen was pledged with two children. Lorol, his pledgemate was content where she was and couldn't see much point in going to a new territory. She didn't want to leave Bacamir so Millen came to Ardena alone. When he asked his mate to come to Solport and try to adapt, she did on two different occasions but couldn't adjust to the different culture and language. She elected to stay in Bacamir: They separated and she dissolved their contract.

Fraya assigned Millen as her mission planning specialist. In that role he helped resolve most of the operating issues, logistics, and scheduling. She relied on his judgment and even kept him involved in technical matters as well as administrative managing.

While the first commercial spacecraft was readying for launch the design and construction of the second craft was already started. Fraya and Rami could see efficiency in using hardware common to the two designs and did whatever they could to make them similar, especially for life support and habitat module accouterments.

A major first markstone was the design, building and launch of the Barge, the staging platform to reach and stay in orbit around Terres. The Barge was unmanned, to be occupied later, and launched for the interplanetary crossing using conventional chemical propulsion. Before the first spacecraft was launched the Barge had to be sent on ahead and parked in orbit around Terres awaiting for the space-pilots to arrive.

Millen had been involved in every major operation for Restor Enterprises including construction of the facilities, mission planning, the launches of flight hardware into local orbit and the actual Terres flights. So naturally he was asked to help decide what specialists should make up the colony for the eventual manned flight. His ideas went into the shaping of a proposed list that he kept on a board in Fraya's conference room. One of the first specialists he recommended was a counselor from Rami's home town, dominary Levey Roch.

Millen had heard much from Rami about the dominary and his impressive credentials and thought he might be an ideal candidate as the psychology leader for the group. He urged Rami to visit his former home and evaluate the dominary as a candidate. Fraya agreed and also urged him to go, so Rami left to visit his home borough and see the dominary.

6. THE DOMINARY

Rami first met Dominary Levey Roch in Lignus, his home borough, when he went there to attend the last rites for Rubel, the daughter of his closest friends. The child had died after inhaling ash from a nearby volcanic eruption, and last rites were administered by the dominary.

Rami had been very impressed with the dominary and made a mental note that this person might be a good addition to the colony if and when he and Fraya decided they needed a counselor on the team. Rami's foster parents, Milda and Jerod Wog, loved to entertain and were anxious to show off their son, now well known from media exposure about the exploration of Terres. Milda planned a party for

20

Rami inviting parents of the deceased Rubel and the Dominary and his pledgemate. Rami entertained the guests by explaining all he could about the first commercial venture, the contact with the primitive tribe on Terres, how the two space-pilots were attacked on the surface and how one had died during the return flight from those injuries.

"What did they do with the body?" Jerod asked.

"They sealed him in his space suit, wrapped him in extra reflective insulation, and jettisoned him into space."

"What happens to the body?"

"We think it freezes and continues to orbit around the sun until it either impacts something or spirals into the sun."

"Can you tell us about the proposal for a colony?" Dominie Roch asked.

"Yes. We were planning on having a second quick-trip with a few scientists to gather more artifacts and do a little scientific research, but the first trip was so successful our investor said we could skip the second quick-trip and get right to the colony. The colony will be a larger group of people who can stay long periods or rotate with some staying while others return to Baeta."

"This next trip you are planning, you call it a colony. How many people will be going?"

"Right now we don't know for sure, but possibly ten or twenty people," Rami replied.

Krysl had been relatively quiet but was getting enthusiastic about the subject. "Will there be any women going?"

"Oh yes. Fraya is going, you know."

"How long will the trip be?" The dominary asked.

"If you add forty arcs each way for the trip, plus surface time of ten to twenty arcs, that comes to over an annur. We haven't decided on the surface activities yet but ideally, if living and survival become

21

feasible, some of the colonists may choose to stay and come home on a later trip. Rotation will be an option."

"What types of personnel will go on this trip?" Levey's eyes were glistening with enthusiasm.

"Right now we are thinking mostly technical people ... and a medical team. We are also thinking we should have a counselor or a psychologist along but aren't thoroughly convinced yet." Rami was baiting Levey.

He took the bait, but tried not to appear eager.

"Do you have candidates for all the positions yet?"

"Not yet. We think if the word gets out that we are looking for candidates our correspondence room will be piled with applications from volunteers and then we'll have to sort through the pile to see if there are any serious candidates. We'd rather make our selections from recommendations on a private basis.....you know, interviewing people with credentials that fit into our profiles and who express an interest in the project." Rami was impressed with himself for leading on the Roches in this manner. *I should have been a politician,* he thought. *Maybe I'm learning some tricks from Arin.*

"Considering possible conflicts within a colony a group will fare much better with compatible couples rather than a mixed bag." The dominary, paused, then he added,

"I am interested. Krysl and I are both young and in good health, and we have no children yet. Krysl is a certified assistant medico. I have credentials in psychology as well as dominance, (which Rami already knew) and would like to interview for a position."

"Well, you certainly sound like well qualified, possible candidates. I think it would be a good idea for you to come and visit us in Solport. You can meet Fraya, and get a feel for the proposed trip. If all seems compatible to both parties, we'll see if we can get you aboard."

Krysl looked dejected. "Well, it may be a while before we can get away. I'm not sure we can afford to make such a long trip without some planning and saving."

"I understand." Rami opened a folded tote, and took out a wallet of travel tickets made out to Levey and Krysl Roch. He also gave them a currency-voucher made out to them in the name of Restor Stellar Enterprise.

"Here are your tickets, with open dates. The voucher is redeemable for currency, for expenses such as moc, hostel, meals or whatever. Come when you can and we will have that interview."

The dominary looked at him for a moment. "You planned on our asking for an interview, didn't you?"

"Dominary, where is your faith. This may have been destined by powers we have no control over." Rami smiled.

7. MILLEN AND MAGGIE

Fraya, Rami, and Millen frequently worked in Fraya's conference room with designing, planning, and reviewing. Millen kept a schedule and status board on one wall and one section of the board was dedicated to listing the specialties desired for Terres flight number two.

Fraya frequently studied the list with absorbed interest, altering and changing names as they came to mind. Once while looking at the list, she saw Millen's name as a specialist and looked up in amazement.

"I didn't know you wanted to go on the ride, Millen."

"I really think deep down, that's why I came here and joined you Fraya. You'll need a mission coordinator to keep track of all activities and that's my specialty. I want to go, and I want my friend Maggie to go along also."

When Millen came to Solport without his pledgemate, he spent some time adjusting and grieving and eventually began socializing. He was attracted to a Prollet security agent with an aggressive disposition who spoke her opinions without reserve, a characteristic Millen laughingly attributed to her flame-colored hair. They did things together his former partner would have no part of; physical things like hiking and cycling, and dancing, and they grew very close. They saw each other frequently, and became social companions.

Fraya was pleased that Millen wanted to be in the colony but couldn't justify Maggie as a contributing member. She had no specialty other than being a top agent for Arin Restor, assigned to keep a protective vigil over Fraya. When Millen said he wanted Maggie along, Fraya balked, and sought the opinion of their counselor, Dominie Roch.

"Fraya," the dominary said, "I think Maggie will be a valuable asset to the group. First, Millen needs a mate and they are already an item. Second, the colony needs a domestic administrator; a hab-manager; a matriarch; somebody in charge and Maggie would be excellent in that role. Her personality is charismatic and at the same time she is assertive. She would be an asset to the group."

Fraya thought about the counselor's suggestion. "Well she certainly was a competent security agent and is a bundle of energy. If Rami agrees it's acceptable to me."

Next to Fraya's conference room was a separate room used for interviews and classes. After screening, satisfactory selectees were further screened in this room, and those found potentially acceptable were promoted to an advanced training facility elsewhere in the

24

factory. The training facility had exercise equipment, intelligencers, and presentation equipment. Participants lectured each other and exchanged specialist information.

"Congratulations, Millen and Maggie. You are among the first admitted to the new training room." Fraya gave them each a hug. Not only had they endured, but they were recognized by the others as leaders. They helped produce a syllabus for the training of all the others.

8. THE FIRST FLIGHT TO TERRES

When they were planning for the first trip, Fraya and Rami had planned to go but Arin mandated the crew be limited to three. Fraya hired Corky to work for her on the commercial project and Corky recruited other pilots he had worked with. The pilots helped design the first flightcraft, and flew many flights to local orbit to assemble the Barge and the spaceship in space. Corky's number one pick for an assistant was Kel who worked with him on the platform and was a social friend as well. Glennick and Caleb were his two other selections; experienced, competent, and easy to work with.

Caleb stayed at home but Kel and Glennick flew with Corky on the first trip to Terres. Fraya and Rami sent three space-pilots to Terres in the spaceship; one to stay on the Barge while the other two went down to the surface. Corky and Glennick went down, and Kel stayed aloft to manage the Barge.

The Barge was designed as a space-port, to stay in orbit and become an integral part of other future missions, if more took place. With its momentum carrying it along, the Barge slowly coasted across the void between the two planets; not in a hurry, but scheduled to arrive and park in orbit before the space-pilots arrived in their faster, nuper-driven craft. The Barge was used as a supply craft and a platform from which a landing party could descend.

Barge's orbit was nearly circular and on-board computers kept it at constant elevation, with a nudge from a boosting thruster whenever it was required.

While on the surface, Corky and Glennick had encountered a group of hostile Terrelings. The two pilots had finished gathering rocks and flora, put them in containers and loaded them into the ascent vehicle as cargo. They had an extra unscheduled light period and received permission to visit the defunct unmanned Settler-Two robotic lander to see why it failed. Arin said he would exchange the information with Centre at some future date if it became an advantage for him.

Settler-Two, now overgrown with brush, was about ten kiloquants west of their landing site and they planned on an easy round-trip in one light period. They had plenty of time to spare before the automatic launch of the ascent vehicle. They made the walk and visited Settler-Two, saw that it had been damaged, took some images and then headed back. On the way back to their spacecraft they found themselves being bombarded with rocks and ducked under a ledge to escape the barrage. Before Glennick could get under cover, he was hit in the head and fell unconscious. After a lull, Corky reached out to Glennick and pulled him under the protection of the overhang. Then, he found himself confronted by screaming, charging, primitive-looking men with spears. He stopped them with noise making grenades and dropped one with a tranquilizing dart.

After the rest were chased away Corky stretched the tranquilized Terreling out and took images and blood samples. He stowed the swabs and blood with the artifacts Glennick had acquired and then carried him back to their craft. He got him up the ladder and inside just before the ascent vehicle automatically separated from the base and lifted off. He had barely gotten himself inside and the hatch closed when the ignition took place and headed up toward the Barge. He and Kel got Glennick inside the spacecraft and ready for the return flight, but Glennick never regained consciousness.

When all signs of life in Glennick appeared gone, Corky contacted Fraya in Cubic and asked her what to do. Fraya felt guilty at having given them the permission to travel on foot to find the defunct Settler but that couldn't be undone. The possibility of an attack by Terrelings was not anticipated. After discussing it among themselves in Cubic, Fraya and Rami agreed the best course of action was a space *burial.* Fraya told Corky to dispose of the body.

"Do you mean stow him and bring him back with us," Corky asked?

"No Corky; it won't do any good to bring him back. We've discussed it here, and our geneticist thinks it's an unnecessary risk. If his body is contaminated with some Terreling viruses, he will just be a carrier. He won't have any symptoms, and we won't be able to de-contaminate him. So, here's what I want you to do: Give him a space-burial, similar to a maritime burial at sea."

"Are you sure, Fraya. We can keep him frozen until we get back."

"I'm sorry, Corky, but that's my decision. Wrap him securely and let him go into space."

Kel and Corky wrapped Glennick in his space suit and reflective insulation, and jettisoned him out of the spacecraft: The first known space burial.

The two of them brought the spacecraft and the artifacts home, completing a financially successful first manned landing on the adjacent planet. They paved the way for the second flight four annurs later; this time with Fraya and Rami aboard.   The first spacecraft-assembly was called the Starflier. This second one would be called the Skyflier.

9. THE SECOND FLIGHT TO TERRES

The first manned flight was history and the factory operations and launch facility had been kept very active getting the second flight organized. Finally, with all decisions made for colony activities, Skyflier was on its way.

Twenty passengers and three pilots were off the pad and coasting in Baetian orbit. First task for the pilots was to get everyone adapted to space flight and settled into the Annex before starting the crossing to Terres. Kel, as main instructor, led the training sessions. He was assisted by Caleb.

With everyone settled and Fraya's nausea controlled, Kel began.

"I know it's crowded in this command module, but we'll have a surprising amount of room in the Annex. It is made of Caleb's rubbery material and has expanded to double its diameter, with many sub-rooms and compartments for our hab-keeping.   It also has an observation room with a clear dome I'm sure you'll all enjoy. The view of the celestrium seen from above the atmosphere is awesome. Anything you've ever seen on the monitor or through a magnifier on the surface will seem blurry compared to the view from our dome.

Caleb and I will go into the Annex now and make the electrical connections. Then we'll come back and continue the training session. You'll learn to move around very quickly."

Kel and Caleb equalized the pressure between the two modules, then opened the hatch, and one at a time each pulled himself through the opening and disappeared into the Annex. When the seals were checked and the electrical connections made, Caleb sent a report to Corky that everything was ready in the Annex.

"All indications from up here say we're solid," came Corky's voice over the intercom. "Pressure has fluctuated slightly but may just be instrument noise."

Kel came out and turned to the passengers. "Listen everybody, the life support system has our atmosphere stabilized in both the Cerebel and Annex, which means we can maintain open hatches and go back and forth between them at will. We will, in general, stay in the Annex. With the atmosphere stabilized we can get out of these pressure suits and move around now." He poised suspended in front of the group and demonstrated the activities as he described them.

"Pull the release ring like I'm showing you to equalize the pressure in your suit with the cabin pressure." Fraya let out a sigh of relief and pulled the ring deflating her suit. The others followed suit, and soon all were deflated

"Next we will remove our helmets." Kel looked around, paused for effect, then grinned.

"Be sure to unfasten your helmet latch before you try to remove it." A few people chuckled at his humorous comment, but Fraya saw several try to twist their helmets without unlatching.

"Now wasn't that easy?" All eyes followed Kel's movements and the passengers tried to emulate him. "Remove the mesh bag from the side pocket on your seat and put the helmet in it."

Zipping sounds ripped through the area as flaps on the mesh bags were pulled loose. The passengers pulled the mesh bags out of the pockets and slid their helmets inside. When Kel saw that all helmets were stowed, he continued.

29

"Now unfasten your seat restraints." The snap of metal latches made a chorus of staccato clicks as the belts were released. Fraya saw her belts merely float out to the side or forward, as there is no *down* in weightlessness. The next fifteen milliarcs were total chaos with people flailing their arms, bumping into each other, and clawing at the air to move to a different position.

"Hang on to a restraint Fraya," Rami coached.

"Rookies," hollered Kel. "Get back into your seats."

Caleb came out of the Annex to help. With a lot more flailing and pulling at each other and Caleb helping, Kel finally got everyone settled with something to hang onto. A few even got their seat restraints fastened.

"Does it seem like you have absolutely no control? Well, we'll fix that shortly. Now unzip your suit like we did in training and float a little way up and out of the suit, but hang onto a restraint. When you get out, sit back down and restrain yourself in the seat again."

For the immediate, Fraya waited for another attack of nausea to hit her stomach but it didn't happen. Whether it was the pills or getting used to the weightless state she didn't care. It just felt good.

"Stow the suit in the mesh bag along with the helmet."

Kel slid out of his suit and as he was folding it for stowage noticed a black, grease-like spot on one sleeve.

I wonder what that is?' he mused. *Must be from one of the connectors. Strange, I don't remember grease used anywhere in the Annex.*

"Fraya, take a look at this." Kel showed her the smear.

"It doesn't look like grease. I don't know what it is Kel. Let's ask Caleb."

"I don't recognize it either," Caleb said. "It looks like dissolved rubber."

Fraya looked at the grease spot on Kel's sleeve again and tried to recall any use of grease in the Annex. Nothing registered in her memory.

"We didn't use grease anywhere in the Annex, Kel."

"Well, there must be something that can make a smear. We'll have to wait and see if any more shows up."

Kel continued to hover above the passengers.

"I'm going to demonstrate the easy way to move around. If you work hard at it or try to force a particular motion you'll be straining muscles against themselves and be exhausted in no time. If you make relaxed, positive movements, it will quickly become so much fun you'll love it." Kel let go of a restraint, pushed off the wall, and slowly floated across the cabin. He did a slow somersault in the middle, and timed the turn so his feet landed against the opposite wall.

"Fraya you're next?"

"Let me watch first, before you call on me, Kel." Fraya said.

Just then, she waved her hand, and sounding distressed said, "Caleb, I'm feeling nausea, again."

"I'm sorry," he said. "Did you take one of the tablets I passed around?"

"Yes, and it helped for awhile, but now I'm sick again." She grabbed a bag and projected into it with a gurgling sound.

"Here," Caleb said, "take another pill. If this doesn't stop it, we'll have Surg look at you."

Fraya briefly wondered if the anti-nausea medication would have an effect on the fetus and considered not taking it. Her stomach was too queasy however, and she wasn't ready to explain why she was passing on the pill.

"Okay, back to the training. Millen, let's start with you."

Fraya was relieved to have Millen and now Maggie take over some of the administrative duties. Before the launch, the couple led ground classes in the training facility, and helped make the selections that were narrowed down to twenty finalists for the flight. And now they were the first to get the space orientation training while in orbit, in weightlessness.

While the rest watched, Millen pushed up and out of his seat and floated toward the overhead of Cerebel. He flailed his arms to stop the upward movement and tried to turn toward a wall to no avail. He ended up against the overhead and Kel grabbed at the opportunity to make a point.

"Millen was doing fine, until he tried to change directions. When you push off, people, do it gently and remember that you will keep going in a straight line until you get to another structure. Only then can you stop or change direction.

"Now, try it again, Millen."

10. THE RUBBER ANNEX

In addition to being a Centre space-pilot, Caleb was a Tribune Chemist and had promoted the use of flexible elastomers instead of metals for spacecraft hulls. His tests on small samples showed many advantages but he couldn't interest anyone at Centre in making a large prototype out of something other than metal. On the commercial project, where Fraya was technical manager, he made a strong argument for using the elastomer as the main material for the Annex, which was designed to be the habitat for the Terres flight. Flexibility, resistance to tear, and rapid manufacturing were his main selling points. Also creating a large module was easier with elastomers than metals because the module could be compressed for launch and then inflated on orbit. When it came time to select a material for the passenger module, Fraya and her design team chose Caleb's elastomer.

Cerebel was docked with the new rubber Annex, and the assembly was sealed and orbiting. Kel kept the rookies in the command module for the present, and was coaching them about moving around in weightlessness. He had Millen in midair, against a wall and was trying to get him back to his seat.

"Try it again, Millen," Kel said.

Millen pushed himself off the wall and floated back toward his seat, but hit it sideways. He straightened himself, gently turned around, grabbed the restraints and then pulled himself into his seat.

"Good job Millen. Maggie, as chief hab-keeper you will have to take each of these people to the Annex and get them settled. You're next."

Maggie had watched the demonstration and saw what Millen had done wrong. She had an easy time catching on to the movements.

"It's somewhat like swimming under water," she said.

"That's partially true except water has a lot of resistance and you can change directions under water. You can't here. That's what Millen was trying to do, change directions and head toward the wall. Swim training might have helped if we had the time, but we didn't. We'll all do fine here after a little practice."

Millen and Maggie moved about the cabin for a time and careened off each other once, but soon moved easily. Before long, Kel had all twenty people comfortably moving around and then turned them loose to practice. He took Maggie into the Annex to show her how the sleeping bags were slung and how people got into them. She adapted quickly and took her assignment as chief hab-keeper very seriously. She moved about with a clipboard and made notes and observations.

"Maggie, I'll send in the rookies two at a time and you can get them settled. I'll send in Rami and Fraya first." Kel moved out of the way and waved for the two to slide through the hatch. Once inside the Annex, Fraya couldn't resist asking Maggie a mocking question.

"How do you like this compared to your old security agent job?"

"What makes you think I'm not still doing my old job?" Maggie replied.

"Nothing would surprise me along those lines. Did you look for bugs in our crew modules?"

"Of course. I may have even planted a few myself. Time will tell."

Fraya was amused and assumed Maggie was not serious. Maggie had been a top agent for Arin Restor and had kept a thorough vigil over her ever since the first bugs were found in her hostel. Fraya had a fleeting thought that Arin may have prompted Maggie to continue looking out for her.

After orientation and some practice, Kel got everyone out of the Annex and back into their seats in preparation for blasting out of the local orbit and on toward Terres.

Before the burn to accelerate the Cerebel-Annex-Propulsor on their way, the nuper engine had to be fired up. The nuper was Caleb's job and he started the reactor as he had practiced, jockeying the temperature up to thrust range. After two more orbits a voice from Cubic told them the board was green and to stand by for the trans-Terres burn. The reactor was stabilized at nearly thrust temperature, and Caleb gave Corky a nod.

"Confirmed green here and at Cubic, Corky. We are ready."

Kel announced to everyone that they were going into the *burn* very shortly, "so stay strapped in your seat for a while yet. Just like on the launch, keep your back straight and head against the backrest."

The enunciator sounded: "...five, four,"...

"Abort ... abort!" Corky halted the count. "We have a pressure drop in the Annex. Cubic, I want it checked out before we get underway."

"All right Corky. We'll review it here also. Continue to orbit."

After a pause the voice in Cubic confirmed the pressure drop. "The pressure is down a little Corky, so we better look for a leak someplace."

Kel and Caleb were headed for the hatch between Cerebel and Annex, when Maggie waved at Caleb and showed him her sleeve.

"When you were showing me around the Annex, I got some black, pasty smears on my sleeve. Here." She showed him the smear.

"That looks like the smudge on Kel's sleeve. Do you remember where we were when you got it?"

"No. We'll have to retrace our movements."

Caleb went into the Annex with Maggie, and followed as she circulated. She tried to remember where their movements had taken them. Maggie opened and reached into a storage bin she had looked into earlier, and jerked her hand back in surprise, covered with sludge.

"What is this?" she hollered.

Caleb looked at it, touched it with his finger and recoiled.

"Its partially dissolved rubber," he said. "The rubber has been in contact with something that is causing it to revert, to dissolve back into its basic form. Who's unit is this?"

35

Maggie looked at her clipboard. "It belongs to Clodea Polosek, the geneticist."

"I must talk to her," Caleb said.

He shoved off and scurried through the hatch, and over to Clodea.

"We have a serious problem Clodea. Something in your storage bin in the Annex is dissolving the rubber. We need your help in fixing the problem, immediately."

Clodea Polosek, a geneticist and research colleague of Rami's, was working with him to characterize the immune system in an effort to prevent pandemic infections from new antigens on Terres. She had developed a general vaccine of inert viruses from the Terreling blood Corky brought back on the first trip.

"Everything in that compartment is sealed, so nothing should be in contact with the rubber."

"Well, that may be, but something is happening. What if one of the samples leaked? What would the fluid be?"

"Most likely a sulfoxy liquid," she said. "It's a chemical used to preserve organs and tissue prior to transplant. I have some in there."

"Has it ever been exposed to uri-prene, the rubber compound?"

"Not to my knowledge. I can't think of any reason for anyone to do that."

Caleb thought for a second, then called Corky. "Commander, we have a chemical loose in the Annex that is dissolving the rubber. We don't know how to stop it or how fast it is working, but apparently air is leaking out through the thinning rubber."

"How big an area is affected?"

"So far, about the size of a dinner plate, and all in one small storage bin."

"Can you seal off that bin?"

"Yes, but that may not stop the dissolving rubber. It's feeding on itself, so it will eventually break out of the bin. The thin area could give us a blowout."

"Get Maggie out of the Annex and seal off the leaking area," Corky commanded. "We have no choice at this time but to halt the mission until repairs are made. Apprise the passengers we are temporarily aborting the burn and that we may have to return to the surface. Then figure out our next steps."

"Got it," Caleb replied. "Maggie's on her way out."

With disappointment in his voice, Caleb announced they were aborting the big burn and why.

Fraya banged her fists against the armrests of her seat.

"How could we overlook a thing like this Rami?"

"This shouldn't have happened," he said. "It's a case of materials-incompatibility. The chemical in a sealed container must have eaten one of the seals. We can't test everything in the celestrium."

"Well, it was your idea to bring Clodea along, and I hope her brain is bigger than her breasts, and more functional. You might try concentrating on her brain for awhile Rami, and you had better figure out a way to fix the problem. Then keep an eye on her activities; not on her mammaries."

"Believe me Fraya, I am only interested in her brain. She's done a great job of producing a generic vaccine for us."

"I know that Rami. I don't know why I felt that twinge of jealously. Must be her figure ... she has one and I don't."

"Fraya, you are so beautiful in so many ways, I'm in awe every time I'm even near you. Anatomy has nothing to do with beauty in your case."

37

"Really? I don't know if that was a compliment or not, but in case it was; thank you. Now tell Clodea to get the problem fixed so we can get on with the trip."

Rami conferred with Caleb then reported back to Fraya.

"Caleb is going into the Annex and assess the damage. He'll take Clodea along and the two of them can decide if the reversion can be stopped and the leak repaired. He can't see any reason for me to be in there now."

Aborting the trip and returning to the surface was a last resort. Aborting from orbit was a simple maneuver compared to getting back into orbit after the trans-Terres burn, so it was imperative to make a fast decision on the extent of the damage. For the present, the pressure leak was slow, permeating through the thinning rubber wall, but the possibility of an explosive decompression was very real and imminent.

Caleb and Clodea, in pressure suits, went into the Annex to examine the dissolving area in Clodea's bin. They closed the Annex hatch behind them and then went into Codea's storage area and closed that hatch also. From there they looked at the gooey spots in the wall of the small bin and concluded the chemical and the samples must be removed and jettisoned.

"If you throw away my semen samples Caleb, you'll have to supply me with some new ones you know."

"Are your frozen samples stored in there?"

"No, the cryogenic storage casket is in a different bin but let's get new samples anyway."

"I can't believe you Clodea. We have people vomiting all over the place, a leaking Annex, and rubber that is dissolving, and your mind is on sex. Is it the science or the collecting that interests you most?"

"Well why don't you just 'wonder', and we'll talk about it later." She tried to give Caleb a squeeze in the crotch but the pressure suit was so bulky the effort caused them both to laugh.

"You have open mikes to my channel," Corky warned. "Clodea, get your mind off sex and on fixing the problem. You are on this trip for science, at Rami's request. If you don't behave yourself, I'll have to keep you in isolation. Understand?"

"I understand, Commander."

"What's the assessment, Caleb."

"So far, we see damage in one small storage unit. We can isolate and remove the chemical, but we'll still have the dissolving rubber to deal with."

Clodea poked at the soft mass with a probe. "The reversion is feeding on itself. I don't think we can stop it so we'll have to remove and get rid of all the softened material."

"Commander, we have to de-pressurize this compartment in the Annex, cut out all the rubber that is reverting, and then seal off the little storage unit."

"Is it do-able, Caleb?"

"The storage unit is small so I'd say yes, Corky. Let's get on with it while we are in here. With your permission I'll de-pressurize this one compartment so we can get to the storage unit."

"Are you both suited and sealed?"

"That's affirmative commander."

"Then go ahead. Fix the problem."

Caleb told Clodea to be ready for a new experience, total life-support in a pressure suit.

"We are totally isolated so we can de-pressurize just this one compartment without affecting the rest of the Annex. We will be in a total vacuum inside a form-fitting balloon so life support will come from our pressure suits. You will find movement is difficult because the joints in the suit don't bend easily but we experience it frequently and it is workable."

Clodea mumbled an affirmative reply that she was ready. Before he de-pressurized the compartment Caleb ordered her to remove the loose chemicals and samples from her storage bin and place them in the plastic bag he was holding. She complied, and when she finished and the plastic bag was closed, he opened a valve to release the pressure in the compartment. Their suits ballooned and stiffened in the vacuum, making movements awkward, but Caleb had experienced it many times on other flights and knew what to expect. Clodea let her arms project out and forward and Caleb laughed at her.

"You look like an icon in a muffin commercial, Clodea. Pull your arms in against your chest, and practice bending your elbows a few times. You'll get the feel."

With Clodea's help, pulling on an edge, he cut around the affected wall of the bin and removed the gooey piece of material. Together, they put the piece in the plastic bag with the chemicals and samples, and tried to push it out through the opening but ran into a resistance. There was a layer of insulation on the outside of the hull that stopped them, so Caleb cut into the insulation and made a slit. Then he managed to eject the plastic bag of materials out through the opening, into the black void, and the storage unit was empty. The walls were smooth except for the hole where the reverted material was removed.

Caleb closed and resealed the hatch on the small storage unit so it was no longer usable. Then he pumped up the pressure in the compartment once again and soon the pressure in the suits normalized to the pressure in the compartment. The suits that he and Clodea were wearing relaxed so they could move normally once again.

"Repair accomplished Corky. Let's hope it holds."

11. THE OBSERVATION DOME

Skyflier was on its way to Terres. Fraya and Rami were first to enter the Annex as residents and Maggie greeted them with a slow somersault to demonstrate her dexterity in the weightless state. She got them settled by their sleeping bags and left them to manage for themselves.

Fraya was interested in the damage to the rubber so Rami showed her the small compartment where the leak had occurred. He explained to Fraya that Caleb and Clodea made a cutout to remove the dissolving material and that the hatch to the little compartment would remain sealed for the entire trip.

"How did Caleb get rid of the chemicals and contaminated material?" She asked.

"The compartment was de-pressurized, all materials put in a bag, and he just pushed the bag out through a slit in the insulation. Then they closed its hatch and re-pressurized the compartment"

"What happened to it then?"

"I don't know. I assume it just floated away."

"I hope so. It's highly unlikely but it could still be hanging around, you know."

"Yes," Rami replied, "but the probability is so small that if it's anywhere near us, when we brake for intercept it'll zoom right on by us and just go into an orbit around the sun."

"Well, that's malfunction number two Rami. I hope that's it. We are already over our quota for this trip."

"Yes, I hope that's it for the malfunctions, but whatever comes up, we just have to use our ingenuity and deal with it."

41

Once they were settled in the Annex, Fraya and Rami often visited the observation dome as did other couples. Turns were taken on a volunteer basis.

The dome was located in a separate compartment with surrounding walls for privacy and adjustable visors to block the sunlight. The view was undistorted with no wavering like one gets from surface observations. At every visit, Fraya gasped at the clear view. The sights of the stars never got tiresome to her.

"Look at the Dipper, Rami. See the bright star that lines up with the two stars that make up the lip? We call it the pole star and that's our guide. We are locked onto that star for navigation."

Rami looked in another direction. "We can see much of our planet now. The curvature is prominent. Like Caleb said, compared to the images on the monitor, this view is incredibly clear. I hope my predictions of planet warming are wrong and our home planet recovers."

From the dome they could see in most directions and the home planet was gradually receding. Each visit to the dome the home planet would appear smaller. In the other direction they could see Terres, the destination, and it appeared to grow as Baeta shrunk.

"Look Rami, we can begin to see Terres as a disk already and the shiny dot off to one side is its satellite. It's Still too distant to discern any features but the blue and white colors are beginning to show."

"Yes," Rami replied. "I can see its colors. Look how our planet is getting smaller and smaller. It is an eerie feeling, just like Kel said. Like our umbilical cords are being stretched and stretched and will snap at some point. "

"You know Rami, there will be Terrelings around our landing site and we may see some of them."

42

"There's always that chance we'll meet some hostiles, Fraya. We have no idea whether they will be aggressive or just curious, but based on Corky's experience, we had better have some plans for defending ourselves."

"Defending, yes, but getting away should be a primary option. We shouldn't be there long enough to start a territorial dispute, but just in case, I think we should be postured for immediate departure at all times; ready to get away if we are cornered. Corky said that most of the aggressors ran away when he threw the noise makers at them, so maybe we can keep them away with our noise-making grenades."

During the first ten arcs, the colonists were enthusiastic about this new experience. They were on a flight through space, seeing the celestrium as no others ever had, approaching a neighboring planet in the solar system that contained life as they understood it, and all were in good health so far. Exercise was important to maintain muscle structure. Pedal machines and elastics for rebounding and resistance were available but Stretch had to prod the people to keep them exercising. They all spent time reviewing technical programs in the intelligencers, and read and read and read, but even Rami and Fraya began to get bored. They had been so involved with the program before launch they had very little spare time to themselves or to devote to each other. Now, coasting along in silent flight, the change of pace and freedom from responsibility were a welcome change.

They slept a lot at first, relaxed and stared out at the celestrium. They also found that floating up to the observation bubble and closing the hatch afforded them a degree of ecstasy they had not fancied possible. Intimacy in microgravity while star gazing was blissfully sensuous. Fraya likened it to having sex in a pool, except you don't have to worry about keeping your head above water.

"Oh Rami, this is wonderful: I'm feeling so complete now."

43

"Complete? When we get back to Baeta, let's pledge and start a family.

Fraya pulled her top garment over her head and exposed her naked torso, then floated out of her bottom garment. Rami eagerly nestled her hollows. They made love again and relaxed.

Fraya had done a pregnancy test on herself, and now knew she was pregnant. She hadn't told Rami yet, waiting for an opportune time, and he sounded like he was receptive to the idea of a family. She decided that this was a good time. They were alone, in private, in the observation dome of the Annex, cuddling, and she told him:

"Rami, it wasn't planned, but apparently the chemical in my implant depleted. I lost track of time and didn't get it replaced. I am pregnant."

Rami, startled, held her at arms length, and just looked at her. "I'm kind of speechless at the moment trying to absorb this. My mind is whirling. We are on our way to land on a different planet and have no idea what to expect. We have no hospital, no medical facilities; so now what do we do?"

"We'll just have a baby, like people have been doing for ages. Besides, the timing will be perfect. We should be back home before the baby is born. It will either be born during the return flight or on Baeta after we land back home."

"You make it sound so simple, Fraya. What if something goes wrong?"

"You've never been a pessimist Rami. Just think positive."

"I'll rally shortly," he said. "It's just overwhelming. Of course I've always thought we'd have children after the flights, so this is just a surprise."

"It's funny Rami, you never spoke of children before. I just assumed we'd pledge and have children when the time was right."

44

"I guess the time is right whether we planned it or not. I must say Fraya, you wear pregnancy very well, and the tiny bulge is beautiful." He patted her abdomen. "You are looking radiant and have never looked more beautiful."

In the weightless state, he easily pulled her to him and wrapped his arms around her. "Will you be my pledgemate Fraya? We can get the dominary to perform a pledging ceremony right here in space."

"Thank you for the compliments and yes, I will. This will be the first pledging in space. Let's find Levey and make it official."

They heard a knock on the hatch. "Hey, are you two going to stay in there forever?" Another couple wanted to experience the privacy of the dome.

Rami and Fraya donned their garments and left the observatory completely relaxed and happy. Their dream had come true so far. They were on their way to visit another planet.

I wonder where the baby be born? she wondered. *Most probably either in space during the return flight or on the surface after landing back home on Baeta. If the baby is born on Baeta after we get back at least I'll be in a hospital. On the other hand birthing in weightlessness would be a unique experience, and the child would become famous as a space baby.* She decided speculating on such matters was a waste of time. The baby would be born when it was ready, wherever she was. She let her thoughts drift toward Terres and getting her coveted space flight.

12. THE TRIP ACROSS THE VOID

The passengers were generally relaxed. They exercised using the treadmill and pedal machines and could bounce when restrained

45

on a trampoline with a flexible harness. Most read and studied on the intelligencers.

Physical examinations went on constantly and for the most part everyone fared well. There were some common infections and respiratory problems among the colonists and some weren't exercising enough, but nothing serious. Surg worried about alien Terreling antigens but the advanced vaccine that Clodea Polosek had developed was making antibodies in the colonists.

The vaccine she made used the naked dna approach and produced a generic vaccine using both Baetian and Terreling viruses. She inoculated all the pilots and colonists before they left. No adverse reactions had developed and blood tests had showed that new antibodies were developing in their systems. Her vaccine was for now, a great success, and no one got sick.

As predicted about half the colonists had some nausea at first but medication helped. Within a few arcs it appeared all of them got used to the weightlessness and even Fraya stopped having nausea.

Word got around quickly that Fraya was pregnant. Everyone on the space craft eyed her with a new perspective, looking for signs of a growing bulge or glowing complexion, and Surg made a special chart for her with a column just for the baby. Both baby and mother seemed to be doing well and the baby was developing normally. Weightlessness seemed to have no adverse affect on fetal development as Fraya had predicted from Centre's tests on pregnant animals.

Surg, as colony medical man frequently reviewed the charts prepared by Stretch, his pledgemate, and Krysl the assistant medico. Charting kept Stretch and Krysl busy and provided a fitness profile on everyone for Surg to review. Stretch was a physical therapist who tracked and charted exercise, and prodded those who were lagging. Krysl Roch, the assistant medico, measured and charted vital signs.

Waste matter, usually contained in one big plastic bag was ejected every few arcs from an airlock. As such each bag became a unique fecal satellite orbiting the sun and Rami chuckled at the thought of a future space ship hitting a bag of waste. He could imagine a jettisoned bag somehow being sucked into a ventilation duct bursting in a cabin and spraying the pilots. A startled pilot might say, "how did that get into the fan?"

After nearly thirty arcs of harmonious travel their tranquillity was interrupted by a squabble between Pylar and Cere, an engineer and metallurgist pledged as a couple. Pylar had a very grim disposition and showed very little sense of humor. He vacillated from being overly-protective of Cere or ignoring her for long periods of time. His moods swung from giddy to suspicious. Cere, considered by many the most physically attractive of the females, was getting bored with the trip and began flirting. She made an exhibition in front of Corky and Pylar exploded into a rage of jealousy. Corky had tempted many women with his wit and handsome features but on this trip he was quite reserved and professional. He even curtailed his usual flirtations with Fraya. Cere had casually floated by Corky, passing very near. As she passed by she paused and raised the front of her loose garment as if by accident and exposed her unencumbered breasts in full view of Corky's gaze. Corky complimented her lovely breasts, then pulled on one of her arms to turn her the other way and pushed her away. He ordered her to cover herself immediately. Pylar saw her floating in front of Corky half naked, but hadn't seen him push her away.

"Why are you acting like such a tart?" Pylar shouted at her.

"I'm not. I just flirted a little to be noticed. Everybody flirts a bit to boost their ego. I sure need a boost being pledged to an engineer."

47

"Hold it," Corky said. "I'm commander of this craft and if I have to put you two in opposite ends of it I will. Pylar, she didn't do anything very wrong and I promptly put her in her place."

Levey came to the rescue. "Pylar and Cere, it is time for some counseling sessions. We still have ten arcs to go on this trip and we have to get along."

Fraya got concerned and privately cornered Corky.

"Corky, what's going on?" she asked.

"Nothing Baby, I assure you. I understand the problems that a little jealousy can create in a group like this and I won't let it happen."

He explained to Fraya what went on and that Levey had taken over to calm things down. Surg, the medico was also involved and had given Pylar a tranquilizer. The potential conflict seemed to melt away for the time being.

13. STRANGE VISITORS OUTSIDE SKYFLIER

On the 30th arc, Caleb was running a periscope scan over the outside of the Annex and Cerebel when he spotted what looked like a bulky bag outside against the edge of the dome. The bag looked familiar. He couldn't be sure but when he zoomed in on it, he thought it looked like the chemicals and rubber they had jettisoned back in Baetian orbit. As the only other person who had seen the bag, he had Clodea look at it. She not only confirmed the suspicion but spotted a rip in the bag.

"Caleb, do you see what I think is a tear?"

Caleb studied it with the flexible zoom. "That's what it looks like, Clodea. If it is, the chemical could be leaking out and contacting the rubber. We could have a problem we thought we had solved, and if it is eating at the rubber from the outside, it could cause a thin spot leading to an inadvertent blowout."

Caleb contacted Corky and told him what they suspected.

"How could that be, Caleb? We left it in orbit back home."

"I don't know, Corky. Apparently it was hooked onto some part of the structure and rode along with us. Question is, now what do we do?"

"If you'll get everyone into a harness, I'll try a rapid roll and see if I can shake it loose. If so, maybe it'll drift away."

Corky tried snapping the craft into a roll each way, and as he reversed directions, the bag seemed to let go. As they were contemplating the dilemma, Clodea let out a scream.

"What is it, Clodea?" Caleb asked.

"Look outside! It's something weird."

Caleb looked out, and saw the outline of a figure clad in a space suit, bumping against the observation dome.

"Corky and Kel, you had better come and have a look at this. I don't know what it is, but it looks like a body."

Kel looked at the object, clad in full space suit with arms outstretched. "Holy Zhu, it's Glennick!" he exclaimed. "We jettisoned him four annurs ago and I thought he'd spiral into the sun by now."

"Could he be alive?", asked Clodea.

"No! He was dead when we pushed him out," Corky replied. "We assume he instantly froze."

"I've done some work with suspended animation," she said; "cryogenic freezing of animals; and I actually revived some of them. So if he wasn't clinically dead when jettisoned, it is not inconceivable that he is alive in a frozen state."

"He was dead I tell you," Kel replied indignantly. "No pulse; no breath."

"Well, I was just supposing ... ."

"Well don't suppose, Clodea," Corky snapped. "That's enough discussion about dead or alive. Let's just figure out what we do now."

"Should we bring him in?" Caleb asked.

"No!" Corky was emphatic. "What would be the point. We'd need new calculations for the additional weight of his body; we don't have room to take him to the surface, and lastly, he is dead! So bringing him in would accomplish nothing."

Caleb grumbled some disagreement. "The weight calculations would be simple and we have plenty of room in the Annex. So, what do we do?"

"Nothing," said Kel. "Corky's right, there would be no point to it."

"Then drop it," said Corky once again.

Just then, the automatic stabilizers activated a thruster and gave the assembly a jerk. Glennick's body floated loose from the dome. His body and the bag of chemicals drifted away from the craft. The pilots and Clodea stared in disbelief as Glennick and the bag disappeared into the blackness.

Kel rushed to Cerebel's flight deck, and swept the surrounding area with radar but couldn't get an echo of any kind. The objects against the dome had either slid out of range or would not reflect the radar. Very strange, Kel thought.

"Levey, we need a conference with you right away," Corky said to the dominary.

He assembled the group and explained what had taken place. The other two pilots and Clodea also gave their versions of what they saw.

"What do you make of it Levey? could it be something supernatural?"

"Corky I don't know what you mean by supernatural. Life itself is supernatural or at least a miracle. The events you saw could keep scientists speculating on how or what, for annurs. Personally I think Zhu interfered with an impending disaster for some reason, and for peace of mind we should just accept what happened as a gift. It was either chance, coincidence, or providence, and each of us can choose an answer for himself."

14. DOCKING WITH THE BARGE

Terres loomed larger and larger ahead of them giving the passengers a sense of impending crash. Corky had been through this before and reassured them all was well; they were just waiting for a program from Cubic to intercept the planet's orbital path, and slow into orbit around it. Finally, they got the word that it was time. Cubic relayed the updated instructions and the intelligencers in Cerebel were programmed accordingly. They were ready for the slowing maneuver.

"Per the plan," he transmitted, "we're swinging the assembly around now for retro-braking with the small Dynamo. Give us a count and we'll hit the button," Corky said.

Interplanetary communications are awkward because of the long, round-trip delay through space for each message. Signals required over five milliarcs to reach Baeta and another five for a reply. The count Corky requested was not really an action command, but rather an initiation of the program now loaded into the intelligencers.

They were turned around and at a precise time, braking thrust from the Dynamo-Two slowed the spacecraft into a large elliptical orbit around Terres. When completed, the intercept burn left the pilots relieved. It was critical. If it had not gone well the craft could have missed Terres and gone on into orbit around the sun.

An arc and several burns later they were near the Barge but above it.   When both spacecraft were on the same radial line or imaginary spoke from the center of Terres Corky dropped to a lower altitude matching that of the Barge and the craft moved closer. They were flying in formation now, the standard rendezvous maneuver. The Barge, with all its gadgetry sticking out in various directions made an ungainly looking arrangement of struts, trusses, tanks, modules, antennas, and sun-absorbing electrical panels.   While they were closing, the crew and passengers donned their pressure suits in case of a collision-rupture or other impact causing loss of pressure.

Corky's skilled hands brought Cerebel up near and when it was aligned with an airlock port on the Barge, he nudged it close. The narrow end of an access tube was deployed under the nose of Cerebel, and slid into a docking ring on the Barge. A loud 'clank' took place and the centering springs compressed but the locks did not snap into place. Cerebel hesitated then moved back as the springs pushed it out of the docking ring.

"No capture on the first try Cubic," Corky transmitted.   "I'll bump it in again."

The capture latches had not engaged. Cursing the mechanical failure, Corky made another try and again the locks did not engage.

"Negative on the second try.   Kel is getting ready to go outside."

Kel got out a breathing pack and was preparing to go out for manual engagement when, on the third try, the reassuring sound of snapping locks pinged through the structure. A relieved Kel grinned when the indicator lights on the panel turned green confirming the locks had engaged.

"Lock is green," he called out, giving Caleb the go-ahead to cool down the reactor. Corky passed on the *capture* news to Cubic.

Coupled together, the Skyflier assembly and Barge now orbited Terres as one unit into and out of the sunlight once every fifteen milliarcs. Rami and Fraya stared at the surface below while the reactor temperature was cooling. In so many ways it looked like home but the cloud patterns were not as heavy and the polar caps were larger. Some of the land masses were visible and the whole planet had a bluish color.

Kel looked out a window. "What a beautiful sight. I didn't get to go down on the first flight but I feel privileged to be going down this time. Caleb, you'll get the next one."

"I know." Caleb finally called out; "nuper is cooled and temperatures in the green. Let's go to work."

The access probe was connected to a passageway from a hatch underneath the cockpit. The crew inspected their pressure suits and opened the equalizing valve. When the hissing ended, and pressures were equal in the Barge and Cerebel, they opened the hatch and shined a hand-light into the passageway. Caleb went through the passageway to the crew compartment on the Barge. Peering in, everything appeared to be just the way they had left it. He floated into the Barge and switched on power for internal lighting. Inside, he circled the entire module looking things over then signaled the other pilots to come aboard. The two of them entered and Corky immediately went to a mesh bag fastened to one wall.

"Here's that wallet I've been missing since the last trip. I hope nothing is missing from it."

Kel thought of the encounter with Glennick's body. "If you find something missing Corky, I don't want to know about it. One strange episode so far is enough for me."

The three of them inspected the equipment and supplies and when satisfied that nothing had degraded they readied for their next task, getting the descent vehicle set to take the colonists to the surface. The descent vehicle was attached to the Barge on a different airlock and had a separate passageway. Once again the crew opened another valve and let the pressure equalize between the vessels. Kel opened the hatches and glided into the lander, looked around and thought about living in this cubicle for awhile.

"This is mighty small Corky. I'm glad we'll have tents to move into. Caleb, you'll have this big Barge all to yourself until we get back."

"Just make sure you get back."   Caleb gave them a farewell salute. "I'll talk to you when you get settled."

15. THE COLONY LANDS

The Skyflier had completed its forty-arc interplanetary trip from Baeta to Terres, made rendezvous with the orbiting Barge   and docked. Corky and Kel readied the landing vehicle for descent, got all the colonists aboard and departed for the surface.   They left the Skyflier on the Barge to use for the return trip to Baeta. Caleb stayed in the Barge as communicator and pilot for the Barge if it needed to be maneuvered.

Rami took extra time getting Fraya positioned in the crowded lander so she was in a semi-prone position leaning back and hands cupped around the prominence at her abdomen.

"How are you feeling Fraya?" Rami asked.

"I'm actually feeling very well, no cramps or pain, and the baby seems to be very active, as if enjoying weightlessness."

"Since we'll be back and heading for home in a few arcs, I am wondering if we shouldn't leave you up here with Caleb, to avoid the stresses of landing and the launch back off the surface."

"Rami, I've been waiting to step out onto Terres since I was a small child, and I'm this close. The baby is doing fine, handling the stresses better than I, so forget about leaving me up here. I am going down with the colony. Period." Fraya left no opening for discussion.

"It was just a fleeting thought, Fraya. Now let's get you strapped in."

Corky remotely activated a homing device on the old base and used it for guidance. He maneuvered the landing vehicle through the skip-cool-skip entry into the atmosphere, steered toward the pre-selected landing site, and settled onto the ground not too far from the base they had left four annurs earlier.

"Looks like home Caleb. The colony is landed and all is well. Please report this to Cubic."

"All right Corky; I copy you down and safe."

They landed in sunlight and moved outside to stretch and move around. Even though exercise in the Annex helped, legs were weak from the light gravity during the flight and some had to kneel down to keep from fainting. The sudden return to full gravity caused nausea and retching in some but it passed quickly. Those who could stand up did, and erected a fabric security tent near the hatch on the lander. The tent, made from flexible rods and tightly woven fabric went up quickly and Rami staked it to the ground. All twenty people and the two pilots gathered around and admired their new surroundings.

Fraya felt a huge sense of accomplishment when the landing vehicle finally came to rest, and she could actually step out onto the Terres soil. Standing on another planet had been her dream since she first looked at the planets through a magnifier, and now that she was here, she stood, closed her eyes and drank in the euphoria of the exploit. Then she got very light-headed as gravity pulled the blood down and away from her head.   Rami saw her knees buckle and caught her, then lowered her to a sitting position. She opened her eyes, slid her hand over her belly and looked down at it.

"Hang in there, baby. We are doing fine, so far," she spoke to the little prominence at her abdomen.

As soon as the security shelter was completed Rami insisted Fraya lay down to rest. She willingly got off her feet and settled onto a pad in the shelter. The rest felt good to her and she found herself drifting, sleepily. There were times during the flight when she had doubts about continuing but Rami was always optimistic and encouraging. She shuddered when she thought back on the break in the fueling line, and how close they came to *abort*, when the Annex material started to disintegrate. The rubber reversion problem was unforeseen, but pilot-chemist Caleb resolved it so they could continue. She heard Corky giving directions to the group gathered outside the tent.

"Sunlight passes quickly here," Corky announced. "We'll sleep during the dark period and will all spend this first dark sleeping in the Lander. When it is light some of us will move to the security tent. Then, by the third light period most of us should have our strength back, and we'll set up our long-hab."

Corky had been on the surface before and told the colonists to expect the sun's rapid movement to be startling. It was. They were all amazed at how fast the sun arced across the sky. A complete period of sunlight took about a quarter arc. In comparison, they were all used to Baeta's slow rotation where the light period and dark periods were each about fifty arcs.

For the first dark period after landing, all the passengers and the two pilots huddled in the landing vehicle to rest for the night. Most slept irregularly in the crowded lander and nudging elbows and knees made sleeping difficult. Cere, the metallurgist was one of the more outspoken among the colonists and was quick to lash out if she felt violated. She was small and shapely, with an ample bosom and when a hand from somewhere in the dark groped her, she called out in a loud voice to her pledgemate:

"Pylar, where are you?"

"I'm against the wall, across from you," he answered.

Dimmed lights in the cabin showed silhouettes only. Features were unrecognizable.

"If you're over there, then the hand that is groping me couldn't be yours." She pushed at it. "It had better go away or I'll beak it."

The hand disappeared and no more crowding or groping occurred.

Pylar, the engineer, was her pledgemate.

"Cere, were you flirting again?"

"I shouldn't even dignify your question with an answer, Pylar, but no! Now stop your shouting and quit disturbing people."

"All right," Corky boomed, "let's all settle down and try to get some sleep. We have a lot of work to do after the sun comes up. We have ten light periods to gather all our specimens, so make the time productive."

* * * *

For three light periods they got accustomed to the new surroundings, regained strength in their legs, and erected some small fabric shelters. First project on the agenda was construction of the long-tent, a habitat of flexible rods and fabric, to use as sleeping quarters and a messing facility. They called it the long-hab, and it was a welcome change from the cramped quarters in the lander. After staying inside for the first two nights with little room to move, plus the added stress of gravity, the long-hab was a roomy haven. Maggie, the habitat manager, arranged so everyone had space for sleeping pads and personal items. So far no one had seen an animal or a Terreling in the area so most of the people slept comfortably in the long-hab, feeling reasonably safe. It was chilly but they were warm in their pads. Most were tired, and sleepy.

16. COLONY ACTIVITIES

People were eager to explore and early the fourth light period they spread out around the fields gathering specimens for the cargo. The landing site was a relatively flat field surrounded by low hills.

Geologists Hecktor and Kirsovich picked samples and placed all those that were similar in the same piles. As they expected, most of the nearby *finds* were similar, and they would have to spread out to scout for different samples.

Larissa and Rubicor were gathering leaves and seeds from nearby grasses and plants and stowing them to classify later. Cere, the metals scio, and Thelana, the minerals expert, examined rocks gathered by the geologists. They didn't find any metal-bearing minerals in the rocks gathered so far.

"We'll have to find rocks that are broken, and not smoothed by erosion," Thelana said.

There were no big surprises in what they were seeing. This was the second manned landing, and the space-pilots on the first trip brought back many images and artifacts with them. The grasses, bushes, and trees were not all that different from what they had on Baeta. Rami assumed plant metabolism would be similar and he pulled a small plant out of the ground.

"As I assumed it has a root system, and a trunk or stalk with capillaries to transport fluids upward. What else could it be? It's the beauty of adaptation at work."

Rami was a bio-scientist, and was also an evolutionist. Seeing similarities in flora on two planets affirmed his convictions that evolution by adaptation works.

The objective of the expedition was gathering artifacts, flora, and minerals, to take back to Baeta. Arvidon, the mining engineer, wanted to do some blasting to get a variety of deeper, different rock species, but had no heavy drilling equipment. He had planned to use existing fissures and cracks in which to plant explosives, so he only brought a few hand tools. His hope was to find a burrow deep enough for a good blast site.

On the fifth light period, everyone spread out to explore and gather as usual. Someone found a small hole in a hillside and alerted Arvidon. It was only a few quants deep but large enough to crawl into with some explosives. He pushed them as far back as he could, wired a remote controlled detonator, and retreated. When the area was clear of people, he fired the charge. A loud explosion ripped open a new section of rock and soil, and enlarged the hole big enough for a person to enter for a short distance. After the dust and smoke cleared, Arvidon walked in, shined a light around, and shouted out "success".

The remainder of the light period was spent with diggers trading off turns clawing at the rocks with the hand tools. With new rock faces and apparent minerals showing up after the blast, Larissa and Rubicor felt new enthusiasm for gathering. The scientists agreed that being here first and examining evolutionary life on another planet, even cursorily as they were doing, was the ultimate privilege in their professional lives.

Under Kel's guidance, the artifacts and specimens were loaded into a robotic transport vehicle to be sent aloft to the Barge. Caleb would capture the transporter and transfer cargo to the Annex for the return trip to Baeta.

"Keep looking and working," Kel coached. "We have five light periods behind us and about fifteen to go."

Each sun, Surg and Krysl examined everyone for any change in body temperatures, hemeo pressures, or signs of infections. They had started the charting in the Annex, before the landing, but now that they were in gravity and in a foreign atmosphere, the environment was all different. Air in the Annex was filtered. Here, the air was loaded with spores, pollens, or other stratisborne respiratory contaminants, and allergies were expected. So far, none of the crew members or colonists had any signs of allergic reactions to what they were obviously breathing or touching.

Surg also frequently examined Fraya very thoroughly, and pronounced her and the baby in good health. The fetus had a strong heartbeat, and was very active. Sometimes a kick from the baby would startle Fraya.

"A few more arcs here, and we'll be on our way home, baby." She had a habit of speaking aloud to her unborn.

"If you are born on the trip home, shall we declare you a Terreling or a Baetian?" She chuckled at the rhetorical thought. All her calculations still put her on Baeta before the birth, but the possibility of birthing during the trip home, in space, amused her.

17. THE TRIBES OF TERRES

The native residents of Terres, at least in the landing area, were generally contented. They hunted, gathered, and picked to sustain their existence, and made caves into shelters. They governed themselves by tribal leaders and council discussions. They mated and paired, and committed to families that raised children. They developed customs and rituals, and believed in spirits. Death was a natural phenomenon they saw in all animals. They mourned their dead, buried them, and committed the spirits to leave and carry on elsewhere.

The Terrelings, as the Skytribe called them, accepted the order of nature as they observed it. So, the cavemen were upset at unnatural events from the sky. Over the last few warm seasons, their Shaman kept seeing a single new light streaking across the dark sky, moving very fast, not like the others that moved so slowly. And, it didn't flare up and burn out; it just kept appearing without much change. Shaman speculated it was the point of a spear that belonged to a Skytribe somewhere; a Skytribe that would sometime come to their area.

And then the Settler, the big insect, or thing they thought was an insect, came out of the sky spouting fire underneath and dangling from big wind catchers. The landing was witnessed by a local tribal leader and some of his hunters. They assumed it was a live insect that would hatch, and fearing it might be dangerous, they set up a vigil of hunter-pairs to watch it. Arg, the tribal leader had approached the thing himself , and when he saw movement of one of the appendages, he beat the thing with his club, and then left it to die.

The hunters who watched the insect, kept up the vigil for a half moon cycle, but began to complain about the assignment. Finally, the leader had a conference with the Shaman and other elders of the tribe, to discuss the object and what to do about it.

"No insect takes so long to hatch. I wonder if it is still alive?" The leader asked.

"Arg," the Shaman began, talking to the leader, "we know little about this thing. Some of the men said they taunted it with their spears and it did not awaken. Some said they tried to move it but it is too heavy. You, yourself, have attacked the thing with your club, without waking it. I think the thing must be dead and the men are getting bored."

Arg thoughtfully responded. "I have heard grumbling from some of the lazy louts. They would rather be playing or hunting. I know they play and hunt while they are out on watch anyway, so I don't see what they are grumbling about."

"I think the problem is lack of action," Shaman said. "Most of our activities like fire tending, guarding, hunting, all involve some action. Waiting for an insect to hatch is like watching for flowers to bloom in the fields. The men need a more lively activity."

Arg thought about the Shaman's idea. "From the size of the thing, it cannot be so fierce that a group of us cannot control it if we must. After all, we have defended against jackals who have tried to rob our meat, and we have killed the woolly mammoth and the cave bear for food and skins. We will leave the thing alone for awhile and see what happens. Besides, it is time to begin preparing for the seasonal cave bear hunt, and the competition with Wigor's tribe. That will raise the spirits of the young men. I will tell them there will be no more daily watching."

Interest in the thing waned, and it was nearly forgotten when another object came out of the sky and landed. It was even bigger than the *insect,* and two strange sky creatures got out of it. The creatures moved about, went to the *insect,* went back to their sky object, then left.

Two of Arg's hunters, who had witnessed the first insect, also saw the lander come down, and the two Sky people emerge from it.

62

Arg was a docile individual, and leader of a passive tribe. He influenced his hunters and warriors to be peaceful, take only game needed for food, and defend their area as necessary.

On the other hand, a neighboring tribe competing for resources, was led by Wigor, an individual notorious for being aggressive and easily agitated.

Wigor had seen Corky and Glennick when they hiked away from their sky object, to find the original robotic lander the natives called the *insect*. Wigor's warriors attacked the two creatures with rocks. Glennick was knocked unconscious but Corky chased them away with noise grenades, and downed one of the warriors with a tranquilizing dart. Wigor was not sure he did the right thing by attacking, and decided to confer with Arg and his Shaman.

Wigor and Arg did not get along well, but Wigor had great respect for the Shaman in Arg's tribe. With a contingent of warriors accompanying him, he went to Arg's cave, waved a peaceful signal to Arg's guards posted outside the cave, and waited for an invitation. The guards alerted Arg to the visitors.

"Wigor is approaching," they announced.

Arg invited Wigor and his men to sit around the community fire, with Shaman and his elders.

"What do you want, Wigor?" Arg asked. He did not trust Wigor, for his behavior was unpredictable. Wigor had been known to lead his pack in an attack on others in rage without much more provocation than a territorial intrusion.

"Have you seen the strange objects and creatures that have settled near us?"

"Not creatures, but we have seen the objects," Arg replied.

"What should we do," Wigor said. "There were two creatures and we bombarded them with rocks. Then we attacked, but they had

63

strange boom sticks and noise makers, and we ran away. One of my hunters was hit in the chest by a boom stick and fell, but he wasn't hurt."

"Why did you attack? Were they threatening?"

"No, but they were in our territory, and we wanted to drive them out." Wigor replied.

Shaman looked at Wigor and raised his hand to make a point. "They have skills we know nothing about. They have materials better than anything we have ever seen. They come from the sky, this tribe, and we should try to learn from them. More creatures will come. So, Wigor, I say leave them alone unless they become aggressive. Then, we'll have another conference. We shall defend ourselves if we must."

Shaman's speech seemed to satisfy Wigor for the present, and he pronounced approval of the plan. They would not attack any more Sky Creatures unless they were threatened. Arg listened to Wigor's word of pronouncement, but he still did not trust him to leave the Sky creatures alone.

Arg's people had eventually found the base that remained after the ascent vehicle left, but of course Corky and Glennick were gone. They examined the object, and the word they carried back to the tribal elders was a second strange object had arrived. Not an insect like the first one, but bigger with two creatures in it. Shaman said he was not surprised.

"I predicted this," he said. "Creatures from the sky were here to look for the big insect, the thing you killed Arg. More will come."

Arg, himself, had taunted the insect, and had beaten it with his club. From then on there were no more noises or movements from the thing, and he assumed he had killed it. They left it alone, except that some of the tribesmen curiously tore at the metal parts and wiring from time to time. Eventually it became an object of little interest, overgrown with brush, and mostly forgotten until the two sky creatures came and looked at it.

18. THE HUNTERS SEE THE COLONISTS

When the big object came out of the sky, three warm seasons had passed on Terres since the first two sky-creatures had come and gone.

Drum and Maug, who had seen the *insect* land years before, had been hunting for several suns and were about to head back to the cave, when the colony's lander arrived. This time many creatures spilled out of the new object.

"It is another object like the insect," Maug said. The two hunters stayed hidden from view across the field and watched as creatures poured out of the object and began to walk around. Some dropped to their knees as if they were too weak to stand.

"Look ," said Drum. "Some are up but on wobbly legs, like a newborn animal."

"Could they be newborns from a big insect? asked Maug. "Some are patting the ground, and picking up dirt in their hands."

"I don't know," Drum said. The two were so curious, they stayed all the light period to observe the activity, and saw some of the creatures erect a clear, plastic bubble by the door of the object. They could see some were gaining strength, and walking in and out of the bubble.

Drum and Maug hurried back to the cave, to tell Arg what they had seen. They skirted around a lake on the way, passed the thing they called the *insect*, and made their way past Wigor's hunting grounds. When they got back to the cave, Arg called the council of elders together to listen. The two hunters described as best they could what they had seen.

"A huge thing came out of the sky with fire underneath, like we saw before from the insect. This thing was much larger than the insect, and had many creatures in it." They described the strange creatures that got out of the thing, how they acted, and the shelters they erected.

"They have come back to get the insect, like we thought they would," Shaman said. "Let us hope they are not aggressive and hostile."

"How will we find out if they intend us harm?" Maug asked.

"We can stay away from them," Arg said, "and let them leave on their own in due time. If we threaten them they will harm us with their loud rocks and sticks. If they are like animals, they will not bother us except to protect their young or territory. Most will not attack unless cornered: A wild dog will defend itself. Even the lowly, fearful rodent becomes aggressive when trapped. Let us assume these creatures are like the animals, and will leave us alone unless we bother them," Arg replied.

"Can we go and watch them?" Drum asked.

"You can watch them if you stay out of sight, and do not threaten them."

"What about Wigor's people. We can't control them."

"I will go to visit Wigor tomorrow, and remind him of our agreement that we would not disturb the creatures. I will remind him that we agreed to just watch them and decide later if they were aggressive."

"Wait," said Shaman. "What if Wigor doesn't know about the new sky object and the creatures yet. Remember, I would like to meet

66

these people and learn some of their ways. Maybe, the Skytribe will leave before Wigor provokes them. Let's not tell him".

19. CUBIC'S ELECTRIAL FAILURE

Communications were passed down from Caleb, as he received them from Cubic. He could usually hear them well, except when he was on the back side of Terres, and then he had to wait out a thirteen milliarcs blackout period.

News was not encouraging from the home planet. With fresh-water supplies diminishing from the atmospheric heating, and territories competing for potable water, civil strife was building. Several suns passed without any word from Cubic, and Caleb said he got nothing, not even a carrier. His call, on the following sun, was even more disturbing.

"Kel, I just received a message from some of our friends on Centre's orbiting platform. Apparently some nuclear weapons have been used by rebellious insurgents, and explosive blasts have destroyed our communications systems in Cubic."

"Where were the blasts?" Fraya asked.

"One was in Ardena near our Solport facility. No blast damage was done to our facilities, but power is out everywhere."

"The weapons were available, so nuclear explosions were inevitable," Fraya said, "and I feared this when we were designing the Cubic building. What I feared most was EMP damage. It can't be repaired. To save time and expense, we didn't shield Cubic's electronics, and we may very well be stuck here, unless Centre's command center can help us."

"What is EMP, Fraya?" Millen asked.

"It's like a super lightening strike. The electromagnetic pulse from a nuclear blast creates incredibly high voltages and current, and in the time it takes to snap your fingers, all unshielded circuitry is burned beyond repair. Cubic had no circuit shielding, and will probably have to be completely rebuilt. That can take annurs."

"Caleb," Corky called. "ask them if Centre's ground control facilities are working."

After a long pause, Caleb responded.

"I did. They report normal contact with their facility which is apparently working, at least for now. There were blasts in the area, but proper wire shielding protected their electronics. Does the name Hirl Lockni mean anything to anybody down there? It seems he has some input as to whether we can use their controllers or not."

"I know of Lockni," Fraya said. "And we are not on the best of terms. I hope we can negotiate with him to help us return home."

"I have to ask," Caleb interjected. "How is the *gathering* going? Are we on schedule and planning to head home soon? I'm ready to go home."

"The *gathering* is on schedule, Caleb. Whether we can head home on schedule remains to be seen. We have to get permission from Lockni to use their controllers to bring us back into the atmosphere at home.

"How do we do that?" Caleb asked.

"Lockni had me framed for alleged treason, and I beat him in court, so I doubt if he would cooperate to bring us home, but maybe a higher authority will help."

"Can you go to a higher authority?"

"Yes, and I will," Fraya said. "The technical director is sympathetic to our cause." *Fraya had almost forgotten that Lockni tried to have the technical director sent to a shelter, but the director had enough friends in high places to get released.*

"Caleb, try to get your friends on the platform to patch me a link to the director, without Lockni interfering."

'I'll try, Fraya. This is Barge temporarily changing channels."

* * * *

"Kel, I have a link to the director for Fraya, and his name is Karlus."

Fraya spoke into a microphone. "This is Fraya, Caleb. Are we on line to the director's office?"

The answering voice said, "Fraya, this is Karlus. Do you remember me?"

"Of course I do, Karlus. First you were a great technical assistant and helped me with many research projects. Then, for some reason you turned on me and planted the recording devices that bugged my conversations, and helped frame me."

"I was forced into doing that by Lockni, and I apologize, Fraya. Now I would like to make it up to you by helping you get back to Baeta when you are ready to return."

"How can you do that, Karlus?" Fraya asked.

"I have access to the control room in Centre's Cubic, and I know how to work all the equipment. Trust me, I can give you a trajectory and the mid-course corrections, and the intercept and landing programs. Lockni will never know."

"I want to trust you, Karlus, but you crossed me once."

"I have wallowed in guilt ever since, Fraya, and hated myself for it. Look at it this way; I want to make amends and have nothing to gain by giving you bad information, but I'll gain my sanity and self-respect back by helping you."

"All right Karlus. This project is now in your hands. We'll plan on departing the Barge in Skyflier in approximately ten arcs."

20. THE COLONY IS STRANDED

On the sixth light period, Fraya attempted to talk to Karlus. The voice she heard was not Karlus; it was a voice that gave her creepy feelings of dispair. It was Hirl Lockni.

"So Fraya, you thought your life was in danger here at Centre and you managed to escape from Bacamir. Then you worked that foolish commercial project, sent a craft to Terres, and made me look incompetent on a multinational scale. And now you want me to help you."

"We need help, Hirl. I have been talking to Karlus and we had an understanding."

"Ah yes, that dear young man. Too bad about him."

"What do you mean, too bad."

"He is no longer with us. He made a coup attempt, trying to have me assassinated, and security stepped in. He fell victim to something lethal."

Fraya clenched her fists, paused, and steadied her voice. "Are you going to help us, Lockni?"

"Of course not. I would but I don't have the time or equipment, so you are on your own."

Fraya told Millen to assemble the colonists, so she could break the news.

"Folks," she began, "You all know we were planning to stay here for a limited time, and we have rations for just that long. Our control building back home has been destroyed, and we are stuck here for now. We will have to make the best of it, and survive by our wits, or die here together. This is our home for at least two annurs, and there is no guarantee that the control building will ever be rebuilt.

"Don't we have return programs in the computers on our spaceship?" asked Cere.

"We do," Fraya replied, "but only for the initial trajectory. The flight needs corrective burns, and the most critical part is intercept, and then slowing and descending to the surface on Baeta. It can't be done without ground control, and our Cubic has been destroyed." Fraya continued. "Centre's cubic is still functioning and I had a link to a technician that would have helped us make corrections and intercept, but he has been assassinated. As far as our cubic, let's assume they've had some sort of simple power failure that can be fixed," she said, mostly for the encouragement of those listening, "and will have power restored before long. Until then, let's conduct business as usual."

She hoped she sounded convincing, but feared the worst. Her motive, with her *business as usual* mandate, was to keep everyone busy; keep them from dwelling on their predicament. It worked at first, but by the tenth light period, grumbling began again, with Cere and Liev agitating for answers.

* * * *

"Millen," Cere requested, "Call everyone together for a review of our situation."

Speaking to the group, Millen reiterated much of what Fraya had said before. "Our rations are limited; We are stuck here for now, and will have to make the best of it. This is our home. There is no other alternative for the present."

"What are we going to do for survival?", asked Liev. "Larissa, you're the botanist, can you tell what is edible?"

"Absolutely not," Larissa replied. "Even flora that looks similar to what we have at home could be poisonous to our systems. We'll have to experiment, and sample in small quantities."

"No, we can't so that either," said Rami. "Some toxins are slow to affect, and can destroy an organ without symptoms several arcs after ingestion. Also remember," he cautioned, "some toxins at home are seasonal, or concentrated in stalk or leaf. We could be unaffected by something one arc, and a few arcs later it could be lethal. We need help from the Terrelings."

"How are you going to accomplish that?" asked Liev.

"I don't know yet," he replied.

"You can survive here if you want to, Rami. Some of us are going to depart." Liev, the nutritionist who was generally quiet and reserved, suddenly evolved into a mutinous agitator.

She stepped over to one side of the group. "Staying here forever is nonsense. " She pointed at Rami and Millen. "Those people are talking about staying as if it's the only way. I say let's leave without them. Is anyone with me?"

There were mumbles of approval for the mutiny proposed by Liev, but no stampede to her side.

"Are you sure?" Praetor asked his pledgemate, and then stepped to her side. He put his arm around her to show his support, then looked in Rami's direction.

"We are going to leave, Rami, somehow," he said.

Nearly all the others moved in Liev's direction and looked angrily at Rami.

Animosity was clearly polarizing the colony. Only Fraya, Maggie and Millen moved toward Rami, and the large shelter now had two different camps of intent. Rami tried to plead with the others, to no avail.

"You are Terrelings for now, people. Accept it, and lets get on with our survival!" Rami said.

Liev looked at the pilots. "Are you for leaving, Corky?" Kel and Corky were standing to one side, in a neutral zone, looking at Liev. Dominary Levey was leaning toward Liev's position.

"Corky, could you take us back?" asked Levey. "I still think Millen and Fraya are being too pessimistic."

"We could get started on the right trajectory," said Corky, "but without Cubic tracking us, we wouldn't know what mid-course burns to make for corrections. We're talking very small angles at intercept, to either enter or overshoot the Baetian atmosphere. Entry is very critical."

"Well, think about it will you?" he asked.

"I've thought about it, of course," Corky answered, "and the prospects are not pleasant. At first I thought we had no choice because I am trained to complete a mission as assigned, and I didn't think any other option existed. But, I am not suicidal. I have refused test flights that didn't make sense, and I have now come to the conclusion that going back to Baeta without control from Cubic doesn't make sense. We could get stuck in space with an overshoot, or be burnt in the atmosphere, and neither is how I want to die. Here, at least, we have a chance for survival.

"Is there no option to navigating without Cubic?" Levey asked.

"Navigating from one planet to the next is not the problem. It is the entry and landing back at Baeta. There is one option, and that is cooperation with Centre and getting guidance from their Cubic."

"Is that possible?" Levey asked.

"We'd need their full cooperation, and if I understand correctly, that Lockni person refuses to help. Any changes will be up to Fraya," Corky said. " I think it's probable we can learn to live off the land, so I'm staying."

"I'm staying too," said Kel. "No use going if there is no place to go."

"What about Caleb?" asked Millen.

"I'll figure out a way to get him down," corky said. "He has Cerebel up there and if nothing else prevails, he can ride it down." *and with no runway to land on, he'll be lucky to survive.*

Liev prodded her pledgemate. "Praetor, you're a pilot. If these losers won't fly us back, can you do it?"

"I don't even know what the controls look like," Praetor said. Liev finally cajoled Praetor to actually climb into the control cabin of the ascent module and look it over. He sat at the controls, and quickly decided it would be insanity to light up and take off, with no directions and nowhere to go.

"Yes, I'm a pilot, but only an amateur. If Corky and Kel say they can't navigate us back, I'm going to agree with them." Praetor scowled at Liev. "And stop being so negative. Accept what our leaders tell us, and let's get on with surviving here." He stepped away from Liev and moved over next to Rami.

With that, the grumbling lessened somewhat, and Liev stopped her agitating. She moved over next to Rami, and said she agreed with Praetor about not trying to leave on our own. Most of the others finally agreed with her, and the mutiny was quelled.

21. THE STEPS TO SURVIVAL

Maggie had already arranged the long-hab so those speaking the same language could communicate about technologies.

Cere the metallurgist could speak the language of Arvidon, a mining engineer.

Arvidon knew enough about geology to understand the geologists, Hecktor, Kirsovich, and Thelana.

The scientists, Praetor the archeologist, Larissa the botanist, and Rubicor a zoologist, had old bones, bugs, and plants in common. Pylar, the engineer, could join in most of the conversations, as could Fraya and Rami.

Millen was an organizer, and worked to get the colonists thinking about survival, and the future with construction and manufacturing ideas.

"Arvidon and Cere, you have knowledge of metals." Millen said. "Pylar, you are an engineer. With your engineering knowledge and the other technologies we have, don't you think we could build a modern borough of our own?" Millen asked.

Pylar replied. "We do have some good technologies, and might possibly use them to our benefit, except for one thing. All our technologies are power hungry, meaning electrical power. Let's face it," he said. "We have a few batteries, some weak solar panels, and all our references are stored in small intelligencers which will be dead in a very short time. We will soon be as primitive as these natives, preoccupied with survival."

"I disagree," shouted Cere. "We have technology in our heads and can build new power sources."

"Maybe so," added Arvidon. "But we have no raw materials, and couldn't refine them if we did. As a mining specialist, I'd need lots of power to produce metals from ores, and we have nothing for tools except a few, light, hand-held gadgets, designed to pick at some small rocks for cargo. I suppose we could make a bellows to produce high heat, and maybe reduce some metal ores if we found some."

Millen's expression lighted with enthusiasm. "Now you're thinking, Arvidon. We can survive and build a new life if we set our minds in the positive direction."

"How many rounds of ammunition do we have?" asked Rami.

"About one thousand, and five small firearms," Corky answered.

"Well, we had all better learn to use slingshots," said Rami, "because the ammunition won't last long. I am good with a slingshot, and can teach others how to use one. My best friend and I used to have frequent contests, and I got to be very good."

Praetor was pessimistic. "Without going into more questions about our supplies, lets face it ... whatever we have is not going to last long. As a believer in adaptation I venture that we are going to live like the people who are probably watching us from the bushes right now. We are not going to a market for food and clothing. These shelters and the lander will deteriorate from the weather very quickly. We will probably live in primitive shelters or a cave, by then, if we can even learn to live off the land. Oh yes, we have one small ax and might build cabins out of logs. Our ancestors did that. But speaking as an evolutionist, I would venture that we will be so preoccupied with gathering food, our technology will be lost by the time our children have children. We will become like these people, because we will be too busy surviving to make it any different. We won't have time to teach our offspring our brilliant technologies. They will develop superior survival skills, but will lose the technology that we have now. Their children will know even less." Praetor looked around, awaiting rebuttal and hoping for some, but getting nothing but silence. Finally, Cezanne spoke up.

"What about our intelligencers and discs of technology?"

Fraya answered that one. "They are battery powered, and batteries will last an annur at the most. Hopefully we can get some technology out of them before the batteries go dead."

"Wait," Millen ventured. "Arvidon is a mining engineer. Cere is a metals specialist. We know how to make a wheel and use a lever, two inventions our ancestors didn't have for eons. We have the advantage of these inventions, and we can start anew."

"We can try," Pylar answered. "but I think Zhu may be punishing us for abandoning our planet."

"What's that supposed to mean?" asked Levey.

"I mean we might have done some things to help the situation, but we didn't. We left, and Zhu is putting us here for punishment."

"I don't think you're right, Pylar," Rami said. "A lot of people tried, and couldn't overcome the apathy back home. I, myself, worked very hard trying to get multinational recognition of the runaway greenhouse. I was part of an environmental group that emphasized education for public awareness, but the public in general, seemed more interested in materialistic toys, than resolution of a problem. The toys were mostly driven by combustion engines and were polluters themselves. A situation is not recognized as a problem until an individual is personally affected. If anything, Zhu is punishing Baetians at home for lethargy, rather than us. We may just be his chosen few, to eventually go back to Baeta and get a fresh start. However, chosen or not, our survival here is up to us, not Zhu. "

Pylar's mood turned negative, and he had nothing congenial in his reply.

"Like I said, we can try, but the facts are, we are going to starve to death, or die from eating something poisonous in desperation."

"No we're not," said Rami. "To survive in the wilds at home, we'd have a good idea about what is edible and what is not, and might possibly stay alive until we were rescued. Here, we'll have to learn somehow, what we can eat and drink. And we aren't in a position where rescuers will show up to save us. Fraya and I are going to have a baby, so I need to find out soon, before our supplies run out." He patted her stomach and smiled. "I'm going to find us a caveman and try to communicate with him. Survival is our new priority. We can forget about gathering any more cargo."

22. RAMI MEETS THE TRIBESMEN

Rami had seen signs of Terrelings when he walked around their field. He found animal bones presumably left from Terreling meals, and piles of feces not fully covered with dirt. He assumed the Terrelings had them under observation and wanted to make contact with them. For the next three suns, Rami walked around the field and up into the nearby hills hoping to see a Terreling. He stopped periodically to study the area with magnivisors, eager to spot one who might be nearby. He needed to make contact, without knowing what he would do if and when that happened. In spite of the urgency of his objective, he couldn't keep from occasionally pointing the glasses upward. Flying from tree to tree were an assortment of colorful winged creatures. He found a feather lying on the ground, and he brushed it against his face, feeling its softness. *Feels just like the flying creatures at home. Praetor thinks they were a major link in the evolutionary chain,* he thought, *and that could very well be here as it was on Baeta.*

The grasses in the field were not too different from those on Baeta and he assumed some of the broad-leaf trees might be deciduous, as they were at home. If the leaves changed color here and dropped, he wondered what the seasonal trigger was for vegetation change. On Baeta, the end of annurlight triggered dormancy and seasonal changes. Here it might be climate.

One animal he spotted was a leg-less reptile. Many like it at home had a venomous bite, and he approached it cautiously, touching it with a stick. It slithered away in a swaying, zigzag manner, and disappeared in the tall grass.

Finally, after scouting for three light periods, some movement caught his attention. Animal or man? He studied the area of movement and saw it; a Terreling. Rami's heart accelerated as he walked to the edge of the field in the direction of the movement. When he got near the area, two men appeared from hiding, and then scampered away. Rami yelled and waved, but they ran ahead and disappeared.

Oh good, he thought, *I'm an idiot, expecting them to run up to me while I'm shouting and waving. A wave may be a hostile gesture.*

He stopped and remained stationary until the sun climbed a bit, to see if they would appear again. They did not, so after a long pause, he continued in the direction they ran. Shortly thereafter the two appeared ahead of him, but again, ran and vanished from sight. Rami found a narrow, obvious path through the dry, sparse underbrush, and persevered. He saw the Terrelings two more times, and both times they ran ahead and disappeared, as if leading him on.

Before he left to find some Terrelings, he had decided that whatever the outcome, if he spotted some Terrelings, he would try to follow them. Fraya was opposed to his leaving.

"Couldn't you signal them some way, and try to make contact here in our field?" She remembered Corky's encounter and was frightened for Rami.

"I can try, Fraya, but I figure it would be about as futile as calling to a wild animal to come close. I think I'll have to confront them in their lair."

"What if they're aggressive, Rami, and something happens to you? Can't we learn to survive on our own?"

"We've been over this, Fraya. The vegetation is fickle, you know that. At home, some of the most beautiful, tempting berries contain the deadliest toxins. Do you want anyone to start chewing on a root without knowing if it's all right?" He answered for her. "Of course not. We don't have enough time or people to learn by experience here, and who wants to be a human experimenter. Given enough time we could watch animals and hopefully we could eat what they eat, but I don't think we have the time. Besides, if we are going to be neighbors with these humans, sooner or later we'll have to make contact and it had better be friendly. I've thought it all out. I'll take a homing device to get myself back, a communicator, and a weapon to defend myself if they get aggressive."

"Why don't you take someone with you, to help?"

"I've thought about that also. Corky might be a good companion since he has experience here, but I don't think it's a good idea. I'll appear less aggressive if I'm by myself, and if something happens, why lose two of us instead of just one."

Fraya choked back a sob as she thought how she might lose him. Rami had matured. Back at the Mizzen Institute where she met him, he was childish, needed her tutoring, and his main interest was sex. He had grown from a self-centered, non-assertive, disorganized thinker to this pillar of strength and leadership.

She knew he was right, but dreaded the possibility of losing him. It took two tries before the words managed to come out. "I love you Rami. Now go get us some Terreling friends."

He explained his plan to Corky and Millen, and encouraged them to stay and keep the mutiny quelled. Naturally they both wanted to go, but Rami insisted the colony would be better off if he went alone.

"I'll keep in contact and let you know what's going on. If by chance I get trapped in a standoff somewhere, like you and Glennick did, I'll call for help. You'll have my coordinates and can come and rescue me."

He normalized his homing device so he could find his way back to the encampment. Then he struck out in the direction he had seen the two Terrelings, picking his way around bushes, trees, and water holes. He would stop periodically to survey the area with the magnivisors, thinking that surely he was being watched and sooner or later would spot some of the tribesmen. After several kiloquants of exploring, he finally found himself on trails that were heavily used. Rami figured he might be getting close to the habitat of these people, whatever it was, but the sun was on the waning side of the light period and he thought it prudent to get back. He stopped occasionally to get his bearings and take in his surroundings, and report to Millen on his communicator. Occasionally, a startled animal would run off, surprising him, and he was awed especially by the multitude of winged creatures in the stratos, which he nicknamed 'featheries'. He spotted another leg-less reptile scurrying away, and followed it until it disappeared into a hole, wondering how it propelled itself. *I've got to start making notes of these observations,* he thought. Then grinned at himself. *For what? To take back to Baeta and show the scienomies there? I wish.*

Rami got back to the colony and hugged Fraya. He told her all he had seen and that he found no Terrelings, but did find some trails.

"They may only be animal paths, but I'll search again on the morrow."

She was happy to have him back at least for one more dark. The grumbling of the mutineers was still going on and was depressing to her. The sun settled out of sight and they cuddled on their pads, anxious, but content with their decisions.

They slept soundly and morning came quickly. Rami jumped up at first light and joined in the feeding prepared by Liev, the nutritionist. Liev still had mutiny on her mind and didn't speak to Rami, but accepted her duties and ladled up portions of rations as part of the job.

Rami was eager to go after the Terrelings again. He said good-bye to Fraya and Millen, then took off in the direction he had traveled the previous light period. Before long he found the heavily traveled paths and proceeded in the same direction. Drum, Maug, and several others in the pack had left the cave in the early morning, heading to the field to watch the newcomers. At a turn in the trail and the top of a small rise, they almost bumped into Rami. They were as startled as he, and turned around and ran. Rami called, but they disappeared. He knew running after them was futile, so he didn't try. He called again, but they were out of sight. Obviously this was a path to their domain, so with trepidation he kept going. Every so often he stopped to communicate on his hand-held with Corky, and let him know what was going on. Corky urged him to be careful, because he had seen aggressive cavemen in action, and said he and Millen would follow behind him in case he became trapped. Rami agreed, and said he would be careful. To himself, he wondered how to be *careful*. It was a trite reply.

Every so often, the Terrelings would double back to look for him, and come into his view. Curious creatures, he thought. *If I can depend on their curiosity, I can use this technique to keep from losing them. I'll just keep following at a steady pace, and see what develops.*

He had no idea what their domicile might look like, but assumed it was either a mud and stick structure, or a cave, and about midway through the last half of the light period, he finally saw it.

This is it, he thought, a cave. I may have to shoot my way out, but I'm not turning back now.

The men had run into the cave and disappeared. Rami approached the edge of the clearing in front of the cave, and looked toward the cave entrance. Here goes, he thought, then pushed the brush aside, peered at the surroundings, and stepped out into plain sight. He spoke into his hand-held.

"I'm at their cave, Corky. It has a large opening but part of the entrance is blocked off by rubble. There is a clearing in front of the cave, and a fire smoldering under an overhang. I'm going to the entrance now." Corky acknowledged, said they weren't too far behind, and had Rami's coordinates.

* * * *

The tribal leader, peering out of the cave, saw the brush on the far side of the clearing spread apart, and the strange creature step out into the open. The caveman moved into a crouch, behind the barrier's edge, clutching his spear in one hand on the middle of the shaft, ready for a thrust. The other hand was loosely touching a nearby rock in the barrier, for balance. Thoughts tumbled around in the caveman's head as he analyzed the intruder; battle foremost on his mind:

83

It looks like a man, but different than any I've ever seen, he thought. *Taller than our kind, and long, thin neck. Its coverings are different, not of animal skins, more like the material of the wind catchers we found near the insect.*

Rami moved in halting steps, scanned the opening to the cave, and then slowly moved toward it. The caveman, out of sight in the shadows, watched the creature stop in front of the entrance, and try to peer inside.

If anyone is in there watching me, it has the advantage of shadow, Rami thought, *and could have easily killed me with a spear by now, if it wanted to.*

"Fraya," he said out loud but to himself, "I'm still alive. I hope the fact that I'm still alive is a sign they aren't hostile."

With heart pounding loudly, he moved up to the chest-high barrier and tried to peer over it, but the shadows were too dark. He furtively stepped to the left, around the edge, and stopped again, just inside. In the diffused light, he could see little at first, so he stood very still and let his eyes adjust. After a brief interval, he began to make out objects in the shadows, and the caveman appeared in his vision just two quants in front of him. His heart began pounding so fast it sounded like drums in his head. Their visions locked and both stared, hardly moving. The caveman flicked his eyes up and down looking the creature over, and Rami stood still while he was being examined.

"No sudden gestures," he sternly reminded himself. He had to make this contact work, for the colony; for Fraya, and the baby. Instinctively, he kept his hand near the holster at his side; he couldn't resist, but knew if he drew and fired the weapon, there would never be a chance for peaceful coexistence with these people.

They stared at each other for a while, studying, and Rami tried to stand motionless despite tickling perspiration creeping down his

Rami meets Arg in the cave

beard and under his chin. He caught himself nervously batting his eyes and wondered if the caveman sensed his fear.

Probably, he thought. Why doesn't he blink? He just keeps staring through those big, bushy eyebrows. He looks like the flat-headed creature in the images Corky brought back from the first trip; the one he tranquilized. Not much of a neck. I hope there's a reasoning brain in that head.

Rami guessed the caveman was comparing his features with those of his own people, and hoped the differences didn't incite hostility. He knew what the caveman might look like having seen images Corky brought back from the first trip.

The caveman can see that I'm taller than him. I have yellow hair, long neck, and straight face, much different than him.

The caveman's nostrils quivered, and Rami assumed he was trying to identify his scent. He knew he smelled of fear, but couldn't help it. As his eyes adjusted to the shadows, he saw this man had partly graying hair, but otherwise looked just like the creature in the images he had seen. Then, Rami slowly removed the knife from his sheath along with a small stick of wood from his belt, and demonstrated carving some strips off the wood. Then he kneeled and laid both on the ground, gestured slowly to the caveman, pointed to the knife, stood, and stepped back a few paces.

The man looked at Rami, and then to the knife. He moved to the knife and picked it up, felt it, and smelled it.

It is made like the hard materials from the insect, but this is sharp, like flint. These are the people Shaman said would come, that know how to make strange things. He does not seem to be threatening.

Time to try communicating. Rami finally pointed to his chest and spoke. "Rami," he said.

The man listened, cocked his head from side to side.

Rami repeated his name.

"Rami." He pointed to his chest, while maintaining eye contact.

"Arrrmy?" the man said.

Rami's chest felt like his heart jumped a beat. He was communicating.

"Rami" he said again. Then he pointed to the man with both palms facing upward, and tried to look quizzical.

"Arg," the caveman replied, and he pointed at his own chest.

Rami was elated. He pointed to his chest and said "Rami", and then to he caveman, and said "Arg".

Arg repeated the gestures and tried to say his name. "Arrrmy," and then "Arg."

Others were beginning to appear from behind outcroppings in the cave, and from the shadows. Arg seemed to introduce some of them.

"Zema" he said, and pointed to his woman. "Drum," and then "Maug".

Rami had made peaceful contact. He nodded to all of them and said their names. "Zema, Drum, Maug."

They all came closer and began to touch his clothing. Rami sat down and crossed his legs, and held very still. Members of the pack gathered around him and felt his hair and face. They touched his clothing and pulled on it. Zema left and came back with a piece of the canopy from the first robotic lander some of the men had seen settle. She handed it to Rami, and he held it up near his chest to show that the materials were similar. Rami was relieved, but cautious. They were being friendly and he had survived so far. He remembered, however, that Corky and Glennick had been attacked without provocation, and hoped he wouldn't unknowingly make some gesture that was threatening. For now, he felt the situation was very positive. He had made friendly contact with these people, and maybe the colony could learn how to survive from them.

23. RAMI SOCIALIZES WITH THE TERRELINGS

.   Rami was in the cave, surrounded by curious Terrelings, and beginning to feel some confidence. What were their habits; were they cannibals? In spite of their apparent friendliness, am I potentially the main course at their next meal?

It was too late to get back to the colony, and Rami figured he was here as a guest for the dark. He walked outside the cave, with most of the pack following him, and contacted Corky on his hand-held. The natives watched his strange action, wondering why he was talking into his hand. He told Corky about the contact, and that so far they seemed friendly.

"You two can go back to the colony. I will spend the dark period here, and try to bring some of these people back with me on the morrow. Tell Fraya I'm safe and that hopefully she will be able to learn some of their words. She's a natural linguist; and learns languages easily." Corky acknowledged.

Rami spent the night in the cave, with hospitality that amazed him. He was given heated food, and herbal tea which made him light headed, and when it was time to sleep, he was given some skins to lay on near the zone in the cave that Arg and his children occupied. Both their children were nearly grown now, but neither yet had a mate. They obviously stayed near Arg and Zema, and lived in the same zone they had occupied while growing up. Arg introduced the girl as Moka, first born, and Omal, his son.

With most of the pack curiously watching his every move, he smiled at them, lay down, and pulled the cover over himself. He was getting light-headed, euphoric, very tired and relieved. He had made a contact and so far detected no hostility. The tea that Zema brought to him seemed to make him giddy, and he grinned easily at everyone. Zema brought over a young female and stood her beside Rami's bedroll, clucking instructions at her. He looked up and saw it was Moka, her daughter, and assumed Zema wanted her to make a welcome gesture of some sort. Much to his surprise, Moka slipped out of her skins and slid under the cover beside him. The pack watched with interest, and Rami realized he had a major enigma on his hands. They were offering him a female. If he refused this hospitality, it might jeopardize the rapport he had established so far. They were providing him with a mate, but the problems were, he didn't know how they mated, and furthermore mating was the farthest thing from his mind. He didn't know if he could.

He was reasonably sure coupling was similar to Baetian species after seeing the image prints Corky had taken of the tranquilized Terreling, but the wrong move might offend the pack.

The young female wasted no time in helping Rami answer his own questions. She listened to some more instructions from Zema, and pushed to roll him on his back. Then she reached through the slit in the front in his coveralls to his groin, grasped, and began massaging his flaccid member. He thought erection would be impossible, and mating in front of an audience too inhibiting to ever happen, but surprisingly enough the beverages made him feel giddy, and the physical massaging began to feel erotic to him. Zema brought over another goblet, and he sat up and drank. It was an intoxicating herbal drink and he felt himself relaxing, and his mind wandering. He was getting an erection, and the female, smiling, increased her rate of massaging and stroking.

He reached over and felt her small, nubile breasts, and the area under them to see if she was bi-mammary, or had more nipples. Some of the ancient species on Baeta had more than two nipples when litter births were common. The female pulled his coveralls down off his chest and arms, and the audience seemed to approve with grins and nodding. Rami's thoughts diffused into a cloud. When he was fully erect, Moka said something to Zema, and with coaching got into a position on top of him. She cooed at him, and took his firm member inside of her, and began moving up and down. Rami closed his eyes and thought of Baetian females, of his pledgemate Fraya, the sexy Clodea, the beautiful Cere. He reached her nubile breasts, fondled them and lost himself in the embodiment of this unreal situation. Then, he burst, to the grunting approval of the spectators. When he finished and detumesced, sexually drained, he wondered how strictly physical it all was, and that it could even happen.

Moka cooed to him for a short time, while touching his face and hair. Rami slept some, with the young female at his side, but was restless. The odors in the cave bothered him somewhat. Many of the cave dwellers relieved themselves in the cave rather than going outside, and the smell of urine was strong. When dawn finally arrived, he was eager to get back to the colony. The giddiness he felt before had worn off, and he was wide awake. When Moka again reached for his member, he gently pushed her hand away, reluctant to do anything in haste for fear of offending his hosts. He touched her hair and face, as she had done to him and that caused her to smile. He stood up and pulled up his garment, then motioned he wanted to go outside of the cave. Those who were awake all followed and joined him around the community fire. When he pointed in the direction he had come from,

Rami meets the Shaman and the Caveman's family

and started to walk, gesturing for them to follow, Zema raised a hand for him to stop. Rami was worried, wondering if he had offended them, wondering what they would do next. He was relieved when one of the women handed him a shallow wooden container with hot tubers and meat.

These are the foods we'll need for survival. When he finished the meal, Shaman came over to him and brought Moka to his side, and put her hands in Rami's. Then he began chanting and dancing around them, and patting their hands. Then he patted Moka's stomach, and chanted some more. Rami suddenly realized, with a sinking feeling what was happening. He was getting pledged in a fertility ceremony. The entire pack began dancing and clapping, and Rami felt helpless. He didn't know how to tell them he had a pledgemate, and even if he could, he doubted it would make any difference to them. They probably were not monogamous, and procreation, not pledging, was the essence of their pairing. Males, he reasoned, could own more than one female.

Arg, Drum and Maug concluded that Rami wanted to go back to the field where the sky tribe was, and they began to lead the way. About half of the pack, including some women followed. Rami wondered about their organization and discipline, and figured Arg had quickly designated who could go and who would stay. They trekked together all the way back to the edge of the field where the colony had settled, and then stopped. Moka had stayed right beside Rami for the entire walk, reluctant to leave his side.

The sun was approaching the western horizon when they got to the field. Arg and the others were fearful of getting too close to so many strange creatures, so they stayed on the opposite side of the field. Rami called to Fraya to come over to them, and when she did he introduced Arg, and said her name.

92

Arg tried to repeat her name. "Shraya," he said with a click of his tongue. She smiled and said "Arg", and thought she saw a slight smile. Rami stepped to Fraya and gave her a warm hug, and she hugged back. Moka stepped up and pushed between them, and gave Rami a hug imitating Fraya. Rami briefly explained that he wasn't sure, but he may be pledged to Moka and they could figure out how to get out of it later. Fraya said she understood, and gave Moka a hug, then pointed to her bulging abdomen and pointed to Rami. Moka grinned and pointed to her own abdomen, and then to Rami. Fraya looked quizzical at Rami, and he told her, "I'll explain later."

As Rami predicted, Fraya picked up some of the Terreling words very quickly, and within a short time, along with gestures and body language, could carry on rudimentary conversation. The pack women who were there gathered around her and patted her belly, to indicate they understood she was pregnant. Others from the colony began to slowly drift over to where Rami, Fraya, and the pack stood. There was touching, smelling, and examining with much clucking and gesturing among the tribe people. Liev kept flinching every time she was touched, but Praetor told her to try and hold still.

"They are just trying to decide if we are hostile, and haven't made up their minds yet."

Eventually they seemed to agree among themselves that the strangers came in peace, and Fraya understood what they said. She translated for the rest of the group, to everyone's relief.

Arg bellowed and motioned for his people to gather around him, away from the colonists. After some animated conversation, all but Moka started to walk away in the direction they had come. Fraya pointed toward the group and conveyed a question to Moka why she wasn't going with them.

Moka pointed to Rami and formed some words with gestures meaning "I am his, to stay here."

"Well," she said to Rami, "this is interesting. I hope you're capable of taking care of two females."

Rami started to explain what had happened, but Fraya stopped him. "Never mind, you did what you had to do. This is not the first polygamous civilization to ever exist, and I guess it won't be the last. Besides, Moka can live with us for awhile, and will be our perfect guide to language and edibles. Later, you can give her away to Corky or Kel. If they don't want her, you might try to give her back to the cavemen, but they'll probably kill you." She paused, and said slyly, "If they don't, I might just kill you myself and save the cavemen the effort."

24. ARG'S DAUGHTER JOINS THE COLONY

Everyone had to perform kitchen duty and at her turn, Fraya took Moka to work with her. The young native gathered grains and roots from the fields, and helped cook. Liev watched and made notes on everything she gathered, especially tubers and bulbs. Stalks on the bulbs had turned brown and were laying over, but the wild, pungent bulbs were easy to dig out of the ground.

Fraya temporarily quartered Moka with her and Rami, and put her on a bedroll between them. Moka obviously clung to the idea she was one of Rami's females, and didn't understand why he wouldn't mate with her, even when aroused.

"Fraya, we've got to make other arrangements for Moka. She still considers taking care of me as part of her duties, and cuddles all over me. I can't help it, but it's sometimes physically arousing. I won't let her couple with me, and she doesn't understand why."

"I can see that, Rami. When I get next to you, she just waits until we finish, then crawls back between us. I've tried to explain that you are mine, but she just nods and smiles. She thinks you don't like her. For now, just let her cuddle, with lots of hugging. I'll figure out something."

Fraya consoled her somewhat, but recognized the girl was lonesome for the closeness of her family. Little more than a child, she was barely through puberty, and at times would spontaneously hug and cuddle with Rami or Fraya without invitation. When Arg and Zema came to visit, she would race to them for clutching and closeness.

Fraya decided it was time to give her away, to one of the unpledged males who didn't have a regular bed partner. When she looked over the list, she found Clodea had already garnered Kel into her fold, and he seemed quite contented. Corky was regularly bedding Larissa, the botanist. Rubicor the zoologist had become an item with Kirsovich, an unpledged geologist. Thelana and Arvidon were already pledgemates, as were Cere and Pylar. It wasn't planned that way when they left Baeta, but everybody had a mate. Everybody except Caleb who was still on the Barge. Fraya had an inspirational thought. I'll match Moka with Caleb.

Fraya called Corky away from the group, and said she needed to talk to him.

"What is it gorgeous. I see you're getting a little bulge in the midriff, and it looks good on you. That's the first sign of a shape you've had since I've known you."

"Well, thank you Corky. And in case you haven't figured it out, its a baby."

"I know that, Fraya. Anything I did to cause it?"

95

"Impossible, unless you took advantage of me some time when I was asleep. Now get real and let's talk about getting Caleb down here."

"I've been thinking about that a lot, of course, and we have two options. First, we could bring him down in Cerebel; and second, we could bring him down in Cerebel."

"Very funny, Corky. Now what is your plan."

"Well, the cargo craft will fly to the Barge robotically, but can't get him down. The ascent vehicle can fly up, but was designed for a one way trip, not down again. I could fly the ascent vehicle up, and bring Caleb down in Cerebel, but if we ever get a chance to go back to Baeta, we need Cerebel to fly the Skyflier. There is an emergency lander we call Emler, attached to the Barge. I could fly up in the robotic cargo pod, and bring him down in Emler. That way we'll always have the ascent vehicle available in case we get a chance to leave this place, and have Cerebel on the Barge ready and waiting. Emler is the only craft that is controllable, capable of entering the atmosphere, surviving the heat, and landing at a predetermined site."

"All right, that's a good plan and I approve. Fly up in the cargo pod, and bring him down in Emler; and hurry up, it's getting urgent."

"Why so urgent, Fraya. What's the big rush?"

"I've got to find a mate for Moka to get her out of Rami's bed; she is getting too attached. Caleb will be her mate."

The dilemma struck Corky as funny, and he snickered, followed by some chuckling, and then he roared with laughter.

"That's your crisis? We're stranded on another planet with limited supplies, and you're protecting Rami's virtue?"

She scowled at Corky, then realized how ridiculous her statement sounded, and started laughing with him. It became infectious, and both laughed so heartily it drew the attention of others

96

around them. Finally getting control, she said, "well Corky, that did come across as a selfish motive, but we need this girl as our link to survival. We've got to make her happy; as a paired-up part of our community, and Rami's not motivated to mate with her. Would you like to pair up with her?"

"I can't do it Baby. Not that I have anything against her, but Flower, that's what I call Larissa, and I are sharing a bed now and I don't want to create any jealousy in our arrangement. Larissa is a wonderful lady." He began laughing again and could barely finish his sentence.

"I don't think we should wait any longer to get Caleb down," Fraya said.

"All right, boss lady. Here's the real plan. We have an emergency descent vehicle still on the Barge, and I'll use it to bring Caleb down. I'll fire up the robotic pod and get it going, and dock with the Barge. Caleb and I will load whatever we can into Emler, the emergency descent vehicle, and if you give us a program, we'll land down here near our camp. We'll forget Cerebel. I'll leave the ascent vehicle on the Barge, and come down in Emler with Caleb. We should be able to get him here within ten arcs."

"I don't want to wait for ten arcs. Let's get down sooner if we can."

"It's a labor intensive effort, you know" Corky said. "We have to break camp here and move all our equipment out of range so it doesn't get blown away when the robotic pod takes off."

"Do you have something else to do that is higher priority?" she asked.

"I hate it when you are so rectitudiness," he said.

Fraya chuckled. "You just made that up, Corky. But even though there is no such word, it did make me laugh. I admit, I've

97

always loved the way you could make me laugh, especially when you are trying to be serious."

"Well, this is serious. That's the best plan I can think of."

"All right, Corky. It's a good plan. Let's get on with it."

Corky called Caleb and explained what was going on. Caleb said he was more than ready to get off the Barge, and agreed with Fraya that the sooner the better.

"I thought you would all be back here before now so we could get under way to go back home," Caleb said. "I expected to see the surface on the next trip, but coming down this trip suits me fine."

25. GLENNICK AWAKENS

Caleb sounded a little panicky on his next call. "Kel, is Fraya there?"

"I'm right here, Caleb. Go ahead."

"Some strange things are happening, Fraya. I had just finished talking to the colleagues on the Platform, when, I heard a voice from behind me that was not from a com system. When I turned around, Glennick was there, floating above me, hovering. My pulse raced, and I think my heart skipped a few beats."

"Glennick? Where did he come from, Caleb? What is going on! Didn't we leave him outside?"

"I'm sorry Fraya. When no one was aware, Clodea and I brought him inside. She wanted to see if he was frozen in suspended animation, and if she could revive him. I was curious and helped. She got him thawed, his pulse working, and blood pressure, up. Then, she apparently got some vital organs functioning. She kept him in her Annex compartment, strapped down, for observation and treatment."

Fraya called to Clodea. "Clodea, you had better come and listen to this. We have a problem with another of your experiments."

"What is it?"

Fraya explained what Caleb had told her, that Glennick was loose and moving.

"Is he awake, Caleb?" Clodea asked.

"Not only awake, but moving around and making vocal sounds. Most of the sounds are not intelligible, but he seems aware of his surroundings. I don't think he is rationally awake, and he is uncoordinated, with jerky movements. He is here in the command module, behind me.

"His autonomous systems are functioning to keep him alive and moving," Clodea said, "but we have no way of knowing if any thinking brain is operating. There is probably brain tissue damage. Reviving him is a little more complicated than reviving a soilworm, but obviously part of his brain is functioning, and he may have memory cells kicking in, to recognize his environment. He may even react to what he sees. I think you are in danger Caleb. I recommend you get him back into the annex and put a restraint on him. Then close the valve on the intravenous feeder attached to his arm."

"He'll die, then?" Caleb asked.

"Yes. For sure this time."

"What is going to happen to me, Fraya?" asked Caleb.

"Corky was going to robotically send a load of cargo up to the Barge in the pod, Caleb. But the emergency vehicle is still flyable, so instead, he'll fly up in the pod, get you and whatever supplies you two can stuff in Emler, and fly it back to this base. For now we are stranded here, and want you here as part of the colony. So, first get Glennick shackled and the valve clamped off, and then we'll work on getting you down."

Caleb turned back to the control panel, facing away from Glennick, so he could put the Barge back on automatic controls. When this was done, he turned again toward Glennick, pushed him back into the Annex and shackled him where he was previously restrained. Then, avoiding Glennick's soulful, partially open eyes, he closed the valve on the intravenous tube feeder and pulled his eyelids down.

"Barge is secured, Glennick is restrained and quiet, and I am ready to come down, Kel."

"I'll pass the word. See you soon, Caleb."

26. CORKY BRINGS CALEB DOWN

It took almost two suns for the colonists to dismantle the fabric shelters and the long-hab, and carry everything to a new location on the other side of a nearby hill. They re-established the long-hab so at least the kitchen and messing facilities were functional again, and bedding quarters were placed similar to what they had before. On the next light period, Corky blasted away in the pod, and into orbit to catch the Barge.

Caleb had resigned himself to the possibility he might have to descend by himself in the emergency lander, with no program in the computer. He knew landing survival was possible, but the landing site could be anywhere on the planet. Finding and joining the colony after that was unlikely.

When Corky caught up with the Barge and docked, Caleb was so happy to see him, he gave him a floating hug.

Corky and Caleb started loading medical and food supplies into the airlock between the Barge and the Emler, as they called the emergency lander. Emler was not very roomy, and both realized they would not be able to salvage everything that was available. Working through the airlock was time consuming and cumbersome, demanding they work in stages. When they figured they had enough for a load in the Emler, they readied to move into the airlock and seal the hatch. Before they got inside the airlock, Glennick appeared again. They heard him speak coherently, as he spoke to Caleb.

"Who are you?" Glennick asked.

"I am Caleb, and I worked with you at Centre on the platform."

"I don't remember you. I only remember Corky and Kel."

Caleb sensed he had to reason with this thing, this man who was getting more coherent and aware as time progressed. He did not know whether Glennick would be rational or hostile at this point, so tested him with questions.

"You remember Corky and Kel? Corky is here, and Kel is down on the surface of Terres at the present time."

"Kel not down. I remember that Corky and I are on the surface. We are being hit by rocks. My head hurts. Then I remember nothing, until I remember they pushed me out of the space craft. I woke up, suffocating, and saw the craft drift away. Then I am suddenly here, and don't know what has happened."

Corky nudged around Caleb and talked to Glennick. "You froze. You were dead and frozen for four annurs, in suspended animation. One of our scios revived you."

"Four annurs? That's impossible. But I don't know where I am now, or what is going on. Why did you and Kel cast me out?"

"You were dead," Corky replied.

"I wasn't dead." He began thrashing his arms about, and pummeling on Caleb.

Corky and Caleb pushed him back and forth between them, until they had him pointed toward the Annex once again.

"Fraya," corky shouted into a microphone, "Glennick's here. Apparently he came out of the coma, enough to function with motor skills, broke loose from the restraints, and thrashed his way into the Barge. Completely out of rational control, he began pummeling at Caleb and me. We pushed him back and forth, and managed to spin him around and push him away. Then, he headed for the console, grabbed some controls and began firing some of the Barge's controlling thrusters. We are abandoning ship."

"Hurry Corky," she replied.

Corky gave Caleb a shove toward the airlock.

"Quick, Caleb," Corky shouted. "Get in Emler."

Caleb dived through the opening in the airlock, and Corky was right behind him. Then Caleb closed the hatch on the Barge side and locked it.

The entire assembly was beginning to rock from the thrusters Glennick was firing. The two pilots managed to pass through the airlock and into Emler, getting a few scrapes and bruises on the way. Caleb spun the catches, and called out "sealed:" Corky undocked from the Barge, and backed off.

They could see the Barge and the Skyflier assembly starting to wobble and rotate due to the random thrusts being fired by the irrational Glennick, and knew the assembly was doomed to fall into the atmosphere and burn. The demise of their spaceport, with Skyflier still attached, meant the absolute end of any possibility for a return to Baeta, even if the control buildings were eventually repaired.

Corky gathered his wits and prepared for the descent. They still had a program in the computer for landing , and Corky, using small thrusts from the retro- rockets, slowed to the skip-cool-skip entry that was now becoming his standard. He guided Emler through a flaming glide into the cool atmosphere. As a glider, he maneuvered to the landing spot, slowed to a circular pattern overhead, then deployed spoilers to get the craft over the compound. With his on-board radar assisting him, the canopies popped open for a gentle letdown.

Back safely on the ground, Caleb was mobbed by the colonists with hugs and backslapping, and the party atmosphere sustained until he asked them to back off so he could get the feel of gravity again.

"I appreciate the warm welcome back to the colony, and believe me, I was getting mighty lonesome by myself up there. Now I must get some rest and restore my strength down here in gravity. Cerebel is gone this time, burned in the atmosphere with the Barge. With Cerebel gone, there is no chance of ever going back to Baeta, so we are truly stranded here. We will survive. Zhu has some reason for all this, and we don't know why we are here. I suspect life on our planet as we knew it was gradually succumbing to lack of water from planet warming, and now we have a fresh start here. I am glad to be a part of it." Caleb went to the long-hab and lay down.

Some of Arg's people were nearby, and came to see the new skyperson. Caleb was aware the colony had made contact with the natives, so was not surprised until Fraya presented him with Moka.

Fraya had been teaching Moka some of their words, and encouraged her to clean and groom herself in the fashion of the colonists. She instructed Moka to take Caleb to the bathing stream, and give him a bath. She did so as a duty, but still insisted that she belonged to Rami. Fraya convinced her that she would be better off occupying the bed of Caleb, and to keep peace, Caleb moved her bedroll to his share of the shelter.

Moka unenthusiastically accepted the new resting place as an assignment. Caleb began to communicate with her and gradually warmed to her company beside him. He communicated gently at first, holding her in his arms and stroking her bare back and buttocks. She recognized and encouraged his arousal as he gradually warmed to her company. After a few darks, and much cuddling, she moved to lay on top of Caleb and couple, as she had done with Rami in the cave. Caleb was very ready and the release was explosive. He thought to himself what an historic event was taking place; an interplanetary mating.

Would the reproductive cells be compatible? or was this some higher form of bestiality. Caleb was aware bestial coupling went on back home, but as far as he knew, no issue was ever produced from an animal and a human. Clodea was the genetic and reproduction expert, and he discussed it with her.

"Caleb," Clodea told him, "the propensity for life to propagate is so strong that male and female cells are like magnets. It's probable cross-specie fertilization does take place, not only between a human and animal, but between various animals, but nature is not easily fooled. Even if an animal egg is fertilized by a foreign sperm, the resulting egg would probably abort very quickly. It's nature's way. If Moka doesn't get pregnant soon, I'll give her an anti-aborting drug, and you and she will have a baby."

"Thank you, Clodea, that is very enlightening."

"You're welcome Caleb, and by the way, we don't have your sperm in the collection, so come to my tent later and we'll take a sample and put it in storage." Clodea grinned and grabbed Caleb by the crotch.

"That's nice, Caleb. Remember, I couldn't do that in the Annex when we had those space suits on."

Caleb began sleeping with Moka regularly, and she was accepting her role as Caleb's mate. Rami decided to perform a mock fertility ceremony to make her feel better. With the colonists as witnesses, he placed their hands together, patted her abdomen, and danced around her and Caleb similar to the way Shaman had done with him. She seemed to accept the ritual, and Moka became Caleb's mate. Levey, as one of the witnesses, said some words to the effect that Zhu would condone the pledging and make it fertile.

27. CLODEA MAKES VACCINE

Before joining Arin's commercial venture with Fraya, Rami had been working for the Graduate Institute in Mizzen as a research assistant. He had been commissioned, within a contract from Centre, to work with Clodea Polosek in her Solport labs to study the human immune system. Clodea had been doing some clever research, and had developed a series of enzymes that would strip the protein coating off viruses, leaving a naked d-n-a core. When injected into lab rodents, the naked virus core triggered the immune system to produce antibodies that would kill or inhibit the antigen as if it had the protein coating still intact. The protein causes the virulence.

Clodea did grow human antibodies in the rodents, and multiplied them many times over. Rami was enthusiastic about Clodea's discovery. Not only could the naked d-n-a technique be an asset to interplanetary travel, he could foresee ridding Baeta of some of the virulent diseases that cause powerful epidemics, viruses too strong for the immune system to manage on its own. He wanted to become as knowledgeable as possible, and followed Clodea's mentoring with rapt attention.

"Rami, it is the protein covering on the virus that causes the problems. The immune system is so wonderfully adaptable, it can usually recognize even a piece of virus and start building antibodies in defense. Naked d-n-a fools the system to make the appropriate antibodies."

Government approvals for human applications required lengthy bureaudrudge, and Clodea wanted to expedite the process.

Using a laboratory back at the Institute where Rami was employed, she used herself as a subject, stripped a very virulent virus of its coating, then gave herself an injection and waited to see if she got sick.

She quarantined herself in a locked room in the lab and left instructions for Rami that if the naked d-n-a failed, he was to spray the room with disinfectant, then incinerate her and everything in it.

They communicated through an intercom, and Rami tracked her temperature and condition for the ten arcs it takes to suppress a virus. It worked, and she recovered to normal activity and bodily functions on schedule.

When Corky and Kel had returned from the first trip to Terres, they brought back some flora, and a sample of blood from the Terreling Corky had downed. Rami brought some of the blood and tissue to Clodea for analysis, and together they found d-n-a in every cell they examined. She also found some antibodies in the Terreling blood samples similar to those in the Baetian human system, and Rami encouraged her to experiment with her enzymes to see if she could grow Terreling antibodies in her rodents. She did, made a vaccine, and gave all the colonists an injection before they departed. The injections stimulated immune systems to render the colonists capable of withstanding the Terres environment, as least as good as the Terreling who generously, though unknowingly donated the sample of blood.

Now that he was interacting with Terrelings, Rami worried about the reverse case, that of infecting the natives with antigens from Baeta, carried by the colonists. He asked Clodea if she could make a vaccine for the Terrelings, and she said she anticipated this, already had some prepared, and brought it along.

"I think I have enough to inoculate all of Arg's tribe, but I want to make some more."

She salvaged her enzymes and enough of the equipment she brought down from the Barge, to set up a crude laboratory in one of the shelters.

Her first patient for the new vaccine was Moka, and Clodea faced the problem of convincing her that putting a needle into her arm was going to help her. By cuddling her, Fraya had developed a bond of confidence strong enough to show her how to bathe and groom in a nearby stream. Clodea asked Fraya to persuade Moka to receive the injection, and it was not an easy task. Fraya had to allow Clodea to do an injection of some sterile water into her own arm to show Moka how easy it was. Moka was eager to please, and finally agreed to the inoculation. With that hurdle behind them, Moka helped persuade her father to receive an injection, and then Arg ordered everyone in the tribe to cooperate. The inoculation procedure for more than thirty tribe people kept Surg, Krysl, and Clodea busy for a complete light period, but they got everyone in the pack protected.

28. THE COLONISTS ORGANIZE

Pylar's dour attitude began to evolve after they left local orbit and the crossing began, but few recognized the symptoms. Levey had not seen his negative side during the screening and training, so Pylar was accepted as a colonist. He was pessimistic about the chances for survival on Terres, and was not enthusiastic about building a new borough and looking for resources. He was barely cordial, sullen, and went off by himself to live in a separate tent as a recluse.

Surg had recognized Pylar's symptoms as a type of treatable depression, and convinced Pylar to take some medications. The meds helped, and began to produce a gradual improvement in Pylar's attitude, but Surg's supply of meds was very limited. Surg wondered if the natives had a natural tranquilizer. Rami told him about the intoxicant Zema gave him at the cave and asked Moka if she could make it. She couldn't, but had Zema bring some to the colony for Surg to try. Surg thought it might be useful as a medicine, an *effective tranquilizer, if used in moderation.* He tried some with Pylar and found a fast improvement in Pylar's attitude. The effect was not long lasting; more a beverage for instant recreational euphoria than a cure for anything, so Surg decided against further intoxicants.

The relationship between Pylar and Cere was hardly civil during the flight, and never got any better, in spite of Levey's efforts. Millen was counting on the knowledge Pylar had as an engineer to help the colony utilize some of its technical knowledge, but Pylar was not very cooperative.

Cere maintained a cheerful attitude in spite of Pylar's indifference; always flirtatious, Corky was her target for teasing most of the time. This made Corky uncomfortable, because he was sharing a bed with Larissa, and felt a loyalty to her. Also, he didn't want to see another flare-up of jealousy such as Pylar demonstrated during the flight. He did his best to ignore Cere's flirtations, but secretly felt egotistical that she had singled him out.

After Corky got Caleb off the Barge, through the flaming entry into the stratosphere and safely back on the ground, the attitude of the colonists quietly changed. Although it was never openly expressed, many, as with dominary Levey, kept the thought that while Caleb was orbiting overhead, there was always a chance that some miracle might occur, and a link with home would be re-established. The loss of

Cerebel was the final severing of an electronic umbilical, and with it, any hope for ever returning to Baeta.

Now that everyone had accepted the reality they were here to stay, Millen declared that a colony government had to be organized, established and affirmed. They knew there would be disagreements from time to time that would need some resolution, so Millen was declared group leader, and Fraya remained chief scientist. With Millen as chairman, an arbitration board was established and three people were chosen. Those chosen were Levey, the psychologist, Cezanne the historian, and the charismatic Kel. The entire colony gathered at the end of each light for a group meal and general discussion. Ideas were exchanged, technical matters presented, and assignments agreed upon.

Cezanne," someone said, "how are you going to do your recording when your paper is gone?"

As with any issue, a vigorous potpourri of ideas flew around the group.

"We will have to make more paper," she said. "I'll find reeds like our ancients did, strip and press them together, and make ink from charcoal and tree-sap." There were nods of approval.

Praetor made a request. "As an archeologist, I have been involved in many digs into past civilizations back home, and at every one I always wished there were more written or symbolic records to indicate the history. I propose that we leave a hard record for our offspring, and future generations, to identify where we came from. We can leave it in three ways; first, on disc along with an intelligencer, but both will probably deteriorate in time; or, we can use Cezanne's parchment which can survive in a dry place for thousands of annurs; or, a record in stone which will be the best. If we make some chisels, a record can be cut into a stone tablet, using symbols to indicate that we

109

came from the second planet. Assuming it will eventually be found by some future scio when technology advances on this planet, we might even be able to warn them of the factors which caused Baeta to deteriorate."

Millen agreed, but said stone carving had to be a low priority compared to basic survival tasks. "Providing ourselves with the necessities of food and shelter, will leave little time for stone carving."

Hecktor, the unofficial spokesman for the geologists, proposed an easier method for record-keeping than chiseling stone. "I'm sure we can find some suitable clay around here, and form it into tablets and pottery. Thelana, you made pottery as a hobby, didn't you?"

"I did," she replied. "But I had a studio with pottery wheels, a curing room, and a kiln."

"We'll have to create a studio for you here," Hector said, being a little incisive. "Would you settle for a lean-to and an oven built up form some of the volcanic rock around here?"

"Of course, but how will we heat it?"

Arvidon said he could make charcoal, and would make a bellows from materials and fabric taken from the landing vehicle.

"We may not make ceramics, but we could surely harden clay. Inscriptions could be made in semi-hardened clay, and then fired to preserve the images and writing."

"I'm willing to try," Thelana said. "Let's find some clay and I'll get started working it. Cezanne, you can write inscriptions in the semi-hard tablets, and I'll fire them. Do we have any artists in the group?"

"I can do some scenery sketching," Cezanne replied. "And most of our scientists can make technical drawings. Before long, we'll have so much information, the problem may be deciding what information is relevant to preserve as a record."

Arvidon was enthused. "After we get the bellows made and some charcoal produced, I can even smelt some iron ore if our geologists can find some."

"Is that possible?" asked Hector.

"Most anything we're discussing here is possible," said Arvidon. "I've seen piles of iron-sulfide, fool's gold, around here, but that's very hard to reduce. Best if we can find some iron-oxide, that looks like rust."

"I've seen some of that nearby. Now how do we refine it?" Hector asked again.

"We start with small quantities, Hector," Arvidon said. "We can build a small blast furnace from volcanic rock, and bring ore here on a drag made with poles and skins. We also need some limestone to gobble up the oxygen in the iron ore. And we need lots of charcoal to keep the reactions going. The reactions are exothermic and once the reduction gets started, we can just keep feeding the furnace with ore, limestone, and charcoal.

The molten iron that pours out of the bottom of the blast furnace is not very pure, so we can further refine it in another furnace."

The colonists worked together for half a moon to build the blast furnace and drag some ore and limestone to the site. The experiment worked, and molten iron began to accumulate near the bottom of the furnace. Arvidon then broke it up into ingots that could be handled, and made some small tools to start with.

"We have accomplished many things in a short time," Millen said. "Cezanne, as historian, record what you think is relevant at first. If in doubt, ask Praetor to help you decide. An archeologist should have an eye for what he'd like to find if he were digging at some future time. Or, you can ask the board for guidance."

111

Several cycles of the big, bright satellite passed, changing from full, to none, and back to full. Tracking the cycle proved to be a good method of recording events, but correlating the cycle with Baetian terms was confusing and cumbersome.

"Now that we are Terrelings," said Millen, "what does it matter how many arcs or annurs take place on Baeta. Let's use the sounds of the natives, perhaps shortening the terms a little, and make our own tracking system."

The colonists decided to dispense with the terms of annur and arc and call each cycle a "moon", as did the natives. A moon cycle was the time from one full reflection to the next. Each rotation consisted of a light period and dark period, that became 'solar', and 'night'; words also adapted from sounds used by the natives. It was an easy adjustment for most of the colonists. Cezanne, the historian, began keeping records with the new system, using moons, solars, and nights, and the orbit around the sun became an annum, instead of annur as was used on Baeta.

29. MAKING A LONGHOUSE

Under Millen's supervision, tempered by much advice given by every member of the colony, they completed a vinewood and dirt shelter, and called it the "long-house". Their tools were minimal, one small ax and a folding shovel, but enough to enable them to tie flexible saplings into a triangular, prism-shaped long-house and cover it with bark and dirt. The fabric shelters were taken down and stowed for future use, if necessary, and the colonists moved into the long-house for protection from weather and predators.

The men took some of the metal from the space crafts, and fashioned a heating and cooking range in the long-house. They also took some light petryl from one of the lander's fuel tanks and plumbed it into the makeshift range for fuel. Knowing the petryl would deplete, they set up the range for burning wood, and gathered a large stock of broken limbs and pieces to store in one end of the longhouse.

The geologists found some clay deposits, and Thelana began working the clay into bowls and goblets. Arvidon made charcoal by roasting wood in a large clay vessel, and Thelana hardened her crafts by firing them in an oven of porous volcanic rock heated by the charcoal.

The geologists found some iron bearing ore, and Arvidon began smelting some iron ingots. He also used the charcoal and the bellows for blacksmithing, shaping the iron into axes, hammers, and chisels. The colony had only one small ax to begin with, and the new tools were a great help in digging, moving earth, and adding structure to the longhouse.

Moka had told Krysl that her tribe not only had a Shaman, it also had a medicine woman who knew of natural remedies. Krysl had learned during her training for medico assistant, that tradition and phylogenous knowledge of natural cures existed in certain cultures back on Baeta. Some was learned, and some instinctive.

Why couldn't the same type of knowledge exist here? Krysl thought.

She asked for the board's approval to leave and visit the tribe with Moka. The medical supplies Surg brought would soon be gone, and Krysl argued the ways of the tribe might be useful. The board agreed she could go, but not alone. A contingent of Krysl, Larissa and Rubicor, went with Moka to the cave to learn the natives' way for medicines. The team arrived back a few lights later, and brought the medicine woman, Zema, and several other women with them. Moka had interpreted and they learned many things from the medicine woman, but in the limited time only a smattering of knowledge was absorbed. Some of the dried herbs were laxatives, some reportedly helped infections and fevers, and some of them were analgesics. Most of the herbs are gathered and dried during the growing season, so Larissa and Liev realized they would have to make many field trips when the weather warmed, and learn to recognize the growing plants.

Maggie continued in her role as habitat manager, but with the longhouse built and organized, had very little to do, so she became a language teacher. She voluntarily launched into other projects and soon had more to do than she could keep up with. She helped Liev with kitchen organization and cooking assignments, and worked with Larissa, the plant scio, to learn about edible plants, roots and tubers from Moka. As stores from the Annex were gradually dwindling, the menu was getting monotonous. The wild, pungent bulbs and tubers Moka gathered became a welcome addition to the bland staples from the colony's larder.

The pungent types were mostly bulbs and were found in different sizes. They were edible raw, cooked, or added as a seasoning. Other tubers, some bland and some spicy, were white, or orange, or had purple skins but Moka said they were all edible.

Liev and Larissa experimented with different combinations for flavor and substance. Other colonists were eager to help Liev and Larissa, as cooking became an art rather than drudgery.

One of Maggie's favorite activities was teaching. During her past tenure as an agent for Arin Restor, she had to be fluent in several languages and, like Fraya, could learn them quickly. So that communication skills would multiply among the colonists, Fraya and Maggie began holding classes, teaching the native words to the colonists as they learned them. Moka was invaluable as an interpreter, and learned enough of the Baetian language to exchange sentences.

Maggie was articulate and learned proficient delivery of the native tongue, albeit the combined language she spoke had a mixture of native and Baetian words. Fraya and Maggie were both from Ardena, and Ardenians spoke a soft language. Rami was Bacamirian, and that language was harsh, but technical. All the colonists spoke both languages as a requirement to be accepted during the selection processes, and since departing from Baeta, a combination dialect unique to the colonists had evolved. Now, they were integrating a third; the native language.

"Fraya," Maggie said, "do you see, as I do, we are lapsing into a useful new dialect that is a combination of all three languages?"

"Yes Maggie, and I don't see anything wrong with that. The object is communication and if the new words help us with that, we are fortunate. It will help the natives, who use a lot of sign language, to better communicate with us."

Good articulation by the natives seemed impossible but Fraya didn't care. Understanding was the goal, and *close* was good enough. Apparently the characteristic of their physical stature that gave them a short neck also restricted the pharynx and the ability to form certain sounds, especially those formed by raising or retracting the tongue, and pursing lips. So Fraya became "Shraya" to the natives, and Rami frequently called her that to tease.

"Shraya, how are you feeling? Shraya, can I get you anything?" She thought it humorous, and retaliated by calling Rami, "Arrrrmy".

"Yes Arrrrmy, may I have some water please."

Many of their sounds were accompanied by a click of the tongue, and occasional barking instead of a laugh, and both were difficult for the colonists to mimic. Maggie became very good at it in a short time.

30. BUILDING THE STOREHOUSE

With Arvidon smelting the ores and shaping the metals, the colony now had an assortment of axes and hand tools. Even Pylar, when he wasn't being moody, surprised everyone and participated. He worked with Arvidon to forge an anvil and some hammers, and showed some pride in helping shape tools. They made rods of iron and forged them into spikes of various lengths and sizes, and Pylar organized the colonists into pairs for cutting logs, to make other buildings, including a blacksmith shop. The blacksmith shop became a busy, noisy place with pottery operations flourishing, and the clang ... clang ... of metal being hammered into shapes.

The colonists now had a long-house for living and messing quarters, and a blacksmith shop, but needed one other structure. They needed a storehouse. They knew the weather would turn cold and wet, and needed a place to store dry wood, tools, and food. Pylar begin directing the construction of the storehouse, and picked straight trees which could be handled by two to four people when cut and moved into place. He decided straight log walls would be faster and more efficient than studs, and would support a roof nicely.

"The walls," he said, "didn't need to be very high."

The group agreed on shoulder height as the acceptable goal for walls.

Pylar's engineering background was useful to make pry-bar levers from long logs, and rollers from short, straight lengths of wood. Using levers and rollers, the storehouse went together quickly. It was a labor of pride and cooperation by most all the colonists, men and women, and grew into a recognizable building in a few lights.

Using the sharpened rods forged by Arvidon, the logs were spiked atop one another, and became the walls of the storehouse.

116

The longhouse built by the colony

Last came the rafters, that were saplings bent into arches, and tied with strips of hide. Some were logs split lengthwise to fashion braces across the timbers, and staked with the metal spikes. Shakes were split from some reddish, straight grained wood they found nearby. and fastened in overlapping manner atop the braces with more of Arvidon's narrow spikes. The roof became a mottled array of shakes and bark. It appeared very functional and would keep out wet and cold weather. Holes were cut for smoke vents, and covered with flaps of wood to keep rain and snow from coming into the holes.

When it was completed, Maggie looked it over and said, "When the cold weather is over, I want the long-house rebuilt to look just like the storehouse."

Nobody objected.

31. LARDER HUNTING

The tribe activity seemed so tranquil, Rami became uneasy. Relations with Arg and his tribe were going so well, he almost forgot about Wigor. The next time Arg and Zema came to the colony, Arg looked very concerned. Wigor had come to Arg, to discuss the annual cave bear hunt, and had seen some of the colonists. He said he felt angered that Arg had not shared the knowledge of the new creatures with him.

"We thought you would be gone back to the sky before Wigor discovered you. Wigor is not very friendly, and he is the one who attacked your people when they were here many seasons before."

"Will he attack us?" Rami asked.

"Wigor wanted to attack and drive you away, but we agreed to do nothing unless you become hostile. I have told him that you are peaceful, and he appeared to accept that. He is a thief, however, and may try to raid your dwellings."

The colony's activities turned to serious preparation for the coming cold season. They had a longhouse shelter, a range for cooking and heating, a pottery factory, and a smelter. They knew about the seasons on Terres from data sent by the initial Terres orbiter, but didn't know how severe the cold weather might be.

Based on stories from Moka and others, they expected freezing and some snow. Liev and Larissa, with help from Moka, coached the group to gather a goodly amount of nuts, grains and tubers, but they needed meat. If they could get close enough, they might bring down an animal using their small weapons, but they hadn't even seen an animal up close. They needed Arg's help.

"I see bones of small animals near your cave, Arg. What kind are they and how do you hunt them?" Rami asked.

"They are floppy-ears," Arg said. "We hunt horse, ox, mammoth, and cave-bear, but the floppy-ear is our main food. There are many around, and we hunt them for fur as well as the meat. We will show you how we hunt the floppy-ear when our tribes get back from the cave-bear hunt."

"What is a cave-bear?" asked Rami.

"It is a very huge animal, twice the height of a man when reared up. It sleeps in a cave during the cold season, and we try to kill one for each tribe as a special ceremony. It is tribal custom, so you cannot hunt bear with us."

"Why is it ceremonial?" Rami asked.

"Spirits. Most of our larder hunting is for horse, ox, or mammoth, and we kill only for food or protection from predators,

119

except for the cave-bear. The killing of ox or horse is done by chasing a herd into a dead-end canyon or over a cliff. Then older, experienced hunters spear the animals for the final kill. Spearing a wounded animal takes a great amount of courage, and quite often results in a hunter becoming hurt or maimed by a crazed animal. But for a cave-bear hunt, a single bear is killed in his cave, by a tribal effort."

"Is it competition?"

"Three neighboring packs in the valley compete, and the pack which kills the largest cave bear wins the skulls from the other two packs. The pack with the smallest bear has to place a leg bone from their small bear through the skull of the largest bear, and present it to the winning pack leader to chase bad spirits away. When a bear is encountered, a group of experienced hunters surround and taunt the bear into standing to full height. Then, young hunters dash in, plunge their spears into the bear, and try to retreat before being crushed by the swing of a powerful paw."

"Every young hunter has to prove himself this way?"

"Yes, but it doesn't always work. Wigor's oldest son was killed at the last annual hunt, before the bear was downed, and that was a sad event. His son was liked by everyone and we all hoped he would take over when Wigor quit as leader. Now his second son, who is more like Wigor, will take over."

Rami thanked Arg for the warning, and said they would be alerted and keep a lookout for any tribesmen they didn't know.

"Arg," Rami asked, "when can we go on a hunt with you?"

"Soon. Our cave bear hunt starts next moon, and we go away for a half moon. We will come and take you on hunt for horse next light period, before the cave bear hunt. There are horses near here. "

"We will bring our loud sticks and help you kill a horse with them, Arg."

"Not necessary," Arg said. "We trap them in a canyon or over the edge of a cliff and kill them with spears. You will see."

At the next light period, Rami and Millen, with several of the colony males, went with Arg and his hunters to the top of a canyon. The hunters split into groups: Some went into the canyon to hide, and others spread out to find the game. Rami's group was told to stay near the opening, and chase the horses down the canyon, where they would be ambushed. By the middle of the light period, some animals were finally being herded toward the canyon. The chasers turned them toward the opening, and on a signal, Rami's group chased them down the slope between the rock walls. Near the bottom, hunters with spears jumped out and penetrated several of them. Four of them reared up on hind legs, galloped back and forth as they shied away from waving hunters, then fell in gasping spasms. The hunters cautiously approached, and when close, used their spears to finish the kills. The hunters showed the colonists how to butcher the animals with sharp flints. Arg had the new knife that Rami had given him, and proudly used it to help with the butchering. Then everyone helped carry the meat back to camp, for cooking and drying.

Chunks of meat were skewered and a big meal of roasted meat was prepared by Moka and Liev. The fresh meat tasted good. All in the colony had a lifting of moods from the protein intake.

The hides were proving to be very useful. The meager supply of clothing the colonists brought along was not designed for very cold weather, and furthermore they were getting threadbare from wear. Moka and some of the pack women showed the colonists how to scrape and dry hides, and form them into clothing. Maggie took over as sewing mentor, and before long, sewing became a community project that even Surg participated in.

The colony's storehouse

"I can sew as well as anyone," he said. "After all, my surgical training included a bit of stitching, you know."

Most of the natives didn't wear foot coverings until the weather became cold, so one of their major projects was fashioning boots. The only boots the colonists had were on their feet when they arrived. They were getting thin, so they eagerly participated in making new foot coverings right along with the natives.

In contrast to the rising average temperatures on Baeta, the northern hemisphere of Terres had an ice pack, and was sending its chill southward. Most of the leaves had fallen and a first light dusting of snow had swept the highest peaks above Arg's valley. Frost arrived, stirring the anxieties of the younger hunters who had yet to prove their courage in the cave bear hunting competition, and the taking of skulls.

32. THE CEREMONIAL BEAR HUNT

Wigor's first son had a winning way with people. He was warm and friendly, with a good talent for reasonable trade and barter. He was not belligerent, and his birthright as eventual leader of Wigor's tribe was eagerly anticipated by the other tribes.

Wigor's second son was more like Wigor. Like Wigor, he was feared and the prospect of his becoming tribal leader was not anticipated with enthusiasm.

After the first son's death, the remaining son was next in line to be leader, but he had to prove himself. He was very young and still had to plunge a spear into a cave bear, a feat he hoped to accomplish on this hunt.

Elders from the three tribes met and planned the strategy. There were no cave bears in the valley, so they elected to follow the same path as before, toward the setting sun to the mountains. They would travel together until they got there, but when they arrived at the snow-line, the tribes would separate, and each would hunt independently for a bear. This was the tribal custom.

Last hunt, Wigor's tribe had killed the largest bear, a feat that was clouded by the death of his son. Arg personally liked the son, and as a gesture of respect and sympathy, his people helped dig a grave for the son and joined in the burial wailing. Wigor had the largest bear, and Arg the smallest, so per custom, amid heckling, hoots and derision, had to place a leg bone from his bear through the trophy skull of Wigor's, and make a public presentation to Wigor. Arg did not want to repeat the humiliation, and threatened his hunters with restrictions if they lost the competition again.

The tribes had all began their preparations for the hunt a half moon ago. All agreed ... the journey was to begin in three lights, and as usual they would be gone for a half moon. The anticipation of the hunt was as exciting as the hunt itself, and young men could be seen everywhere practicing thrusts into an imaginary bear. Not every male in the tribe could be included. Some were left behind because of guard duty, old age or infirmary, but no young male wanted to be left. Arg's son Omal had participated in the kill last hunt and had proven himself, so he was now in the ranks of the men who taunted the bear and helped in the final kill, rather than having to make a first thrust.

Three lights went by. The bear hunt was underway. In spite of swirling snow intermittently blocking out visibility, the sun would periodically poke through the clouds and warm the hunters bodies and their spirits. The packs had reached their destination in good weather and spread out into three different directions as planned. Then a snowstorm started one light period after they arrived, and intermittently kept up for a quarter moon. The hunters always welcomed a light snow because it helped them in their tracking, but this heavy fall kept covering all signs of tracks and made the tracking more difficult than usual. Arg had planned to track several bears and be selective, taking the largest, but now he was beginning to fear they might not find any, or worse, get trapped in heavy snow. They had planned to stay for a half moon at the most. Their time was almost up and they hadn't seen a single bear. He wondered how the other packs were doing, and dreaded hearing that Wigor might have already gotten one. Finally, after several light periods and a snow pack that was knee deep, the weather cleared. The packs had an agreement to meet at a lower altitude regardless of their results, and the time had come to start down.

Discouraged and disappointed, Arg's pack marched single file through the snow, starting downward. Before leaving the snow-line, however, Arg recognized a cave where they had successfully killed a bear once before. Several hunters crept inside and found a young bear in a drowsy state, and taunted it to stand up. Even though it was smaller than Arg wanted, they killed it and drug it down the mountain toward the prescribed meeting place. They got there before sundown, and found no signs that either of the other two tribes had yet arrived. Arg's vivid imagination had him visualizing Wigor's tribe dragging an animal so huge it was slowing their travel. He was much relieved when at the next light period, both packs came trudging down without a bear. Neither had even seen one, so Arg became the unchallenged winner of this season's bear hunt. He kept his own bear-skull this time.

33. THE ENCOUNTER

A new life for the colonists was beginning, and Rami had great hopes for their survival now that peaceful contact with native inhabitants had been established. The colonists had built shelters, were learning to hunt and gather, and were refining some metals. The first Terres baby was on its way, and the colony was intact, although not yet in harmony.

If the natives could cope with the changing seasons, so can we, Rami thought. *We can learn to cope.*

The cold season was not far away, and deciduous leaves were losing their green color. Rami finally connected the changing season with the gradually shortening light periods, and the chilling atmosphere. As the warm season seemed to be ending, tall grasses everywhere were laden with seeds, ripened and brown. Moka's people relied on tubers, seeds, nuts and berries for supplementing their meat diet, but didn't realize the small seeds from grasses and grains would grow if put back into the ground. She curiously followed Larissa in her quest for harvesting grains, and when Liev began grinding some of the seeds to meal and cooking them in hot water, she tasted and understood. Not only did she grind some grains into meal, but Larissa planned a big cultivation project for the colonists, when the cold season passed. They were going to become farmers. She tried to explain to Moka about planting, but it was a difficult concept to make known. Liev demonstrated putting seeds into the ground and covering them with soil, but to Moka, that seemed a foolish waste.

"She will just have to wait for the revealing of sprouts at the next growing season," said Liev.

Larissa, planning on some experimental planting during their short stay, had brought along several types of seeds, including large, yellow kernels from a cob, and golden grains from the bread staple of Baeta. She even brought along a few seeds from melons.

The original itinerary called for only a short stay, and Larissa didn't expect to see any sprouting from her seeds and kernels while they were there, but she planned to let nature take its course. She would have been pleased to have images and reports of sprouted plants and grains brought home from the follow-on colony when it arrived. *Now,* she thought, *my crop, if the sprouts survive the weather, may well aid in our survival.*

Pylar slipped into a low cycle of his depression, and his dour moods had an adverse effect on everyone. While feeling good, he had moved back into the long-house, but before long had dropped back into another round of depression and moved back to a separate tent by himself. No one, not even Cere, tried to talk him out of it this time. Levey continued to counsel him, but he was worried Pylar's negativism might even dampen his own zest for life. His defense against Pylar's pessimism was simple; he limited his time in talking to Pylar to very short intervals, and spoke only of Pylar's accomplishments.

Surg had recognized Pylar's symptoms as a type of treatable depression, and convinced him to take some of his medications. The antidepressants, along with Levey's counseling, began to bring Pylar out of his depression to the extent he began to converse more and more with the other colonists, much to the relief of Levey, who had been counseling him. One light period, Pylar marched over to the others, and proudly showed off his achievement. He had made a bow from a strong, flexible, vinewood with a narrow, straight-grained trunk, and a string of thin horsehide. With arrows from the same type of wood, he demonstrated how skillful he had become, practicing on his own. He had killed a small, fur bearing animal and brought it to the group. Moka was excited and said it was floppy-ear, and good to eat.

"The skin is very useful. The fur is beautiful, fine, and soft. If you can get more like it, I will make a cover for Fraya's baby when it arrives."

Enthusiasm is more infectious then depression, and Pylar's bow caused other colonists to heap him with praise. His attitude brightened and he passed a smile onto all around him. He gushed with engineering explanations to the point of repeating himself, and getting groans from his listeners.

"The natives are good with spears, but the accuracy and distance are limited by the motion of the arm as a sling," Pylar explained. "With a simple pull of the bow, the arrow can go twice as far with very little effort. We call it mechanical advantage."

Millen was ecstatic and asked Pylar to gather as many wood specimens as he could while the weather permitted, so they could make more bows and arrows. Pylar showed Arvidon and Praetor the grove of vinewood he used for the bow, and together, they gathered some more straight grained specimens to take back to the longhouse to dry. They made more bows and the two, under Pylar's mentoring, became proficient marksmen with bow and arrow.

Pylar took Praetor on a hunting expedition with bow and arrows, with the objective of finding some floppy-ears. Rami stayed to fuss over Fraya, who was getting big with the baby, and make her a chair. He made a reclining chair with a vinewood frame, and webbed with horsehide so she could lean back at an angle. She found the chair comfortable once she was settled, but it was too low to easily get in and out of. That is where she needed help, and Rami was more than eager to assist her. Some of the other women encouraged Rami to go hunting with Pylar and Praetor.

"Go along, Rami, if you want to," Liev said. "We can look after Fraya."

"Thank you, but I have another project to work on," he said. Rami wanted to practice with his slingshot. He admired the innovation of Pylar's bow and arrow, but realized it was limited by the availability of arrows, which were labor-intensive to make. His slingshot used rocks which were plentiful, and he had gotten very accurate. However, he had yet to kill a floppy-ear with it, and wanted to practice around the campsite.

Pylar and Praetor took bedrolls to the vine grove to hunt for floppies. They had planned to spend only one dark period, but did not return the following solar. After three solars without any sign of them, Praetor stumbled back into the camp without Pylar. His head had bruise marks, and he had been bleeding through his jacket. Surg and Krysl rushed to him and asked what happened. While Praetor mumbled the story, they removed his bloody tunic, and Surg flashed a light into his eyes.

"You have a bad concussion which is affecting coordination on one side of your body. You also have a broken upper arm on that same side. It is compound and very ragged. We will have to set it, and give you medications to prevent infection."

Surg gave Praetor an injection to relieve some of his pain, and let him finish the story.

"Pylar showed me where the vine wood was growing and what to look for. Then we ventured north, hunting for more of the furry animals, and saw several of them. Pylar had gotten two of them with his arrows, and was stalking a third when some natives appeared, and started yelling and throwing rocks. I was hit in the head and arm, and ducked down and hid behind a log. Pylar stood up and shot an arrow into one of the warriors who was near, and hit him. They threw a barrage of spears at him while he stood, and several found their mark. He fell to the ground and was motionless, obviously hurt very badly. The warriors came rushing over to where he lay, and I stood up and fired my sidearm into the nearest one. The noise and shock stopped them, and they turned around and ran. I had no idea Pylar was going to stand up and shoot the arrow, or I would have fired sooner. The warrior Pylar wounded with an arrow ran off. The warrior I shot with my sidearm is dead. Some of the spears hit Pylar." Praetor paused. "Pylar was killed by the spears. He is dead."

A stunned group was gathered around listening to his story. Cere was in a state of shock at the news. "I can't believe he is dead," she wailed. "We don't even have his body for a burial."

"We'll get it and bring him back, Cere." Millen put an arm around her.

"Wigor did this," said Moka. "They went into Wigor's territory. He is mean and just looks for any reason to fight. Now we must worry that he is angered and will come and attack us all."

"I hope that's not the case," said Millen. "We don't have much ammunition left. If they do attack our compound, they will use their spears and clubs as weapons. All we'll have is our slingers, and they won't be good at short range."

With Praetor moved into the longhouse and Liev fussing over him, Millen gathered all the males except Surg into a huddle.

"We have to get to Pylar's body and give him a burial," he said. "How shall we go about this?"

"Praetor can't show us where Pylar is," Rami said. "so he'll have to tell us where to find him. We'll just have to search until we do."

"What about the hostiles?" Arvidon asked.

"We still have a lot of noise bombs, "Corky replied. "We'll have to scare them away."

"Do we have to bring the body back here?" One of them asked.

"No." Levey replied, "but it would be best if we did, for closure."

"Then let's get on with it, and not delay any more," said Corky. "I'll take five others with me. Six of us can make a sling with two poles and some canopy cloth, and we should be able to handle him easily. We'll take some firearms and grenades along in case we are attacked."

"We can assume," Millen said, "Wigor's people will retaliate immediately to avenge the death of their fallen warrior, so he might attack your group, Corky. Be ready for a defensive stand."

"We don't have much choice right now," Corky replied. "We'll have to shoot if the smoke grenades don't chase them off. Sidearms are all we have for defense.

"I'm sure Wigor retrieved the bow and arrows near Pylar's body, and if he figures out how it works, will eventually make some of their own. Isn't it ironic," Millen continued, "The new weapon we developed, so useful for hunting, now may be used against us. Any weapon, in the wrong hands, becomes a threat. We'll have to come up with a defense against it, a weapon to defend against their bows and arrows."

The six men departed immediately. When they got to the vinewoods, Pylar's body was not immediately evident, but the general area Praetor described seemed to fit what they were seeing. They found a large log similar to that Praetor said he used as a shield to hide behind, and visualized the scene of the attack.

"Praetor stood here." Corky found some spent shell casings and concluded Praetor had stood in this very spot to fire at the attackers.

"If Praetor was here," Corky said, "and Pylar was in front of him, then the body should be between us and that ledge. Fan out and look for him in this general area. It is possible the body was moved, either by Wigor or animals, so it may not even be here."

"Where do you suppose the attackers came from?" Levey asked out loud to no one in particular.

"I would assume they were on that ledge and jumped down to this level," Hector said.

Levey spied some large, noisy, winged carrion circling an area to the left, with much screeching as they landed and jumped and flapped back into the air. He moved to observe the activity, and spied Pylar's remains. The body had been dragged to the left of the area they were standing in, and some of it had been ravaged by whatever found it.

"This is not a very nice sight, everybody, but here he is. Presumably some carnivores found him before we did, dragged him over here, and began feeding on the remains. Then the winged carrion began competing, and, well ... let's get him wrapped and on to our carrier."

The body was carried back to the compound, and a grave was dug. Moka, with Arg, Zema, and some of the other tribal members helped lay Pylar's body in the grave, and then performed a wailing ceremony before covering it. They waved their arms into the air, and Moka said it would send the spirit on its way. Levey was amazed, and discussed the event with Krysl.

"Apparently the Terrelings believe in a spirit and bury their dead, Krysl. That leads me to believe the concept of life in spirit form may be more celestial than we think. These so-called primitive people, in a unique civilization, on a planet separate from ours, with no influence from our other planet, believe in spirits. Could it be that a spiritual concept is probably prevalent everywhere in this celestrium, or at least in this solar system."

"I think that is a comforting thought, Levey," Krysl said.

After the attack and death of Pylar, the colony stayed alert to the possibility of Wigor's people attacking again. Corky took the group to the vinewoods, found and recovered Pylar's body, but saw no hostiles.

Three lights later, the compound was attacked by Wigor and ten of his warriors, but revenge was not the motive. Apparently, some of Wigor's people had been watching from hiding and saw the colonists making and using clay pots and goblets. They wanted some of the clay utensils, and came to get some. Wigor was not a barterer, so he didn't ask. He just attacked and stole them.

Some screaming warriors descended on the compound, and grabbed some pots and goblets. The colonists assumed they were there to avenge the death of Wigor's warrior, and countered using noise grenades and slingshots to slow the attack. When the warriors continued to advance, Corky, Rami, and Millen raised their firearms and fired into the group. A few of Wigor's warriors were wounded and one of them was hurt seriously enough to fall, immobilized. He was knocked down in the compound, and couldn't run away like the others. Surg looked him over and decided the wound could be treated, so had him carried into the longhouse, and placed on a bedroll. Then he removed the slug, and stitched the wound.

"If all they wanted was some clay pots," Rami said, "we could have shown them how to make them. I'm afraid we now have a tribe that is antagonized. Millen, I think you had better set up a watch to warn of any more surprise attacks. Also, we all better learn to use a slingshot.

"You are right Rami," Millen replied.

"When the wounded warrior gets better and mobile, we can show him the pots, give him some, and send him on his way."

"We got by with our noise makers and sidearms this time, Rami, but we need a better defense, especially when we have no more ammunition. I have an idea for a defensive weapon that would be better than a club or spear," said Arvidon. "Our bows and arrows are primarily long range weapons. They use clubs and spears, so we also have to use clubs and spears to defend ourselves. But we have an advantage. We have metals and the forge, so we can make a better weapon. I'll make some *swords*, like those used on Baeta in the historical past for close combat."

34. TERRELINGS AND BAETIANS ASSOCIATE

Arg, Zema, and the medicine woman visited often. They looked at the ailing Praetor who was feverish and incoherent, and asked what happened.

"Wigor's people," said Liev. She was beside Praetor, consoling him. "You didn't know Pylar was going to stand up. Don't blame yourself. Just cooperate with Surg so you can get better soon." She gave him a hug.

Without consulting Surg or Krysl, Zema and the medicine woman put a poultice of comfrey on Praetor's arm. Krysl had learned a little about aboriginal medicine when she was obtaining her certification, and told Surg it might help. Surg was aware that natural medicines can be very potent, so made no objection. As a matter of fact, he hoped it worked so they could add it to their arsenal of antibiotics.

The wounded warrior was also convalescing in the longhouse, and the medicine woman covered the bullet wound and stitches with a poultice.

Praetor began to improve almost immediately and his fever started to subside. The poultice on the warrior's wound healed so quickly, he was up and about, ready to leave in a two lights. Arg, however, posted guards near him to make him stay a little longer.

Fraya, in native language, convinced him to stay long enough to learn the methods of pottery making, but he was suspicious of Arg's guards. Fraya had the guards back off, and Arvidon showed him how they made the clay utensils. Then Arg scolded the warrior for being unfriendly and aggressive, and ordered him to leave. The warrior left, disappearing over a hill, carrying several pots and goblets.

Before he left, Fraya told the warrior to come back if they wanted more pottery.

"Hopefully," Arvidon said, "Wigor's tribe would recognize the generosity, and gift giving, as a friendly gesture."

Several moons passed, and Fraya was getting bigger and bigger with the baby.

Although it was mostly a one-way process of learning, before long, Fraya had begun exchanging many sounds and words with the natives. They were communicating. One of the women even let her hold her baby, an ultimate gesture of acceptance and honor.

Rami envisioned many ways the colonists could improve the way of life for the natives in exchange for learning their survival skills. He demonstrated the bows and arrows Pylar had made, and showed them how to lace sharp flint or obsidian points on their spears. He also showed them his slingshot, and Arg was so impressed, he quickly learned to sling a rock.

After the medicine woman and Zema tended to Praetor and the warrior, they went over to Fraya and examined her.

"Baby on way," said Zema.

"How do you know? I have no pains," Fraya responded in Zema's language.

"Baby moving, feel here." She placed Fraya's hands on her bulbous abdomen. Several of the pack women gathered around her clucking advice, and when Surg tried to get into the circle they pushed him away.

"Woman's job," they said. Nevertheless he stayed close in case Fraya needed him. A short time later the first contractions started, and Fraya let out a yelp, startling Rami who had just returned from an outing and his first kill with his slingshot. He had planned to proudly prance into the shelter and show Fraya, but when he heard her yelp, he threw the animal aside, pushed through the circle of pack women and went to Fraya's side. She was starting to perspire and he wiped her brow and upper lip. "I love you Fraya, and I'm sorry I got you into this mess."

"What mess? You didn't get me into this, we came together." Her breath was labored. "And now, we're going to have a baby. Isn't that wonderful."

"This longhouse sure isn't a hospital and it's not very fancy."

"Rami, people have been doing this for millions of annurs and we'll manage just like they have in the past."

The solar wore on and dusk began to fall. Rami looked to the west. It was clear tonight, and Baeta began to show bright and shiny just above the horizon. He swallowed hard and clenched his fists.

"Baeta still beckons, Zhu, but I know its not home anymore. I don't know why all this happened, Zhu, but if its possible, let Fraya be safe." He was talking mostly to himself, and to the evening sky, but felt better addressing Zhu's name.

"We have the essentials of food and shelter. If we can overcome the elements and disease, we'll be all right."

Rami thought, *if prayer helps, then this is the nearest thing to a prayer I've ever uttered.*

* * * *

Amidst the clucking and fussing of the medicine woman, along with Surg and Krysl, Fraya strained and moaned. Rami paced back and forth nearby, outside the fabric shelter, until after dark. Finally, as he thought he might go crazy with the waiting, he heard the cry of a newborn. He went inside and saw Surg looking over the infant, and then hand it to Zema. Zema covered it with a wrap of cloth from the wind catcher, and laid it on Fraya. Rami went to Fraya with tears in his eyes, and she looked up.

"Here's your daughter, Rami," she gasped, "healthy and beautiful. She paused, wondering if Rami had an opinion on a name. "Do you have a name in mind for her, Rami?"

He had already thought of a name, but hadn't yet discussed it with Fraya. The first time he saw Levey was at the last rites for the daughter of Feydor and Raychek. Rubel, the child, had died from inhaling volcanic ash, and Dominary Levey was delivering a eulogy. He spoke of the child's spirit going to another world.

"In light of recent knowledge that life does exist on a world other than this one, perhaps Rubel's spirit will emerge somewhere, on another world."

We are on another world, he thought.

"Fraya, in memory of my friends, Feydor and Raychek, let's name her Rubel."

Fraya thought for a milliarc, nodded, and agreed. "All right, Rubel it is."

Rami lay down beside her and joined in her dreams. They cuddled and watched while Rubel wriggled on Fraya's breast, her light hair beginning to frizz as it dried. She showed much strength for a newborn, and searched for a nipple.

Rami was euphoric. If the colony could make it through the cold period, they would survive. Other children would be born. He visualized generations of offspring eventually pushing the technology to newer and newer heights as they had on Baeta, but will they do it without making weapons to use against one another? He hoped so.

Eons from now, scios digging into ancient civilizations, may find our encampment and stone records. *I wonder if they will understand their heritage, and learn from the mistakes we Baetians made.* Then he corrected himself and said, "those Baetians."

He looked down at Rubel and for the moment, didn't care.

35. THE PREGNANT COLONISTS

With Praetor convalescing in the longhouse, Surg took stock of the medications and general health of the group. The stock was nearly depleted. He had used much of their anesthetics and antibiotics on Praetor, and was counting on getting some of the natives natural medications.

"We will survive," Surg announced. "We will! After all, we have some of the most knowledgeable talent in the celestrium right here: Rubicor, a zoologist, Larissa; a botanist, and Krysl a certified medical assistant. If you add Clodea and Rami to the team, you are awesome. Now, this team will have to figure out what the Terrelings have that works as medications, primarily analgesics and antibiotics.   I'm convinced you will."

Surg privately expressed some concern to his mate. "Stretch, we have a very limited supply of medications. Praetor, alone, has taken a good share of what we had. We are fortunate we haven't had a hostile attack on our compound, either by humans or animals. If such does happen, we could run out of medical supplies very quickly, and be at the mercy of the environment. The comfrey and poultices from Zema were helpful but we need to learn how to make them."

Stretch agreed the situation was critical. "They have a Shaman and a medicine woman. Why don't we learn their ways. They've been doing this for a long, long time and probably have a storehouse of knowledge about natural pharmaceuticals. "If you can spare your assistant Krysl for awhile, perhaps a team of her, Larissa, and Rubicor could go to their cave and learn their ways."

"That is a good idea. Levey, as Krysl's mate, would have to agree to let her go, but that shouldn't be a problem. Let's discuss this with Millen and tell him our concern. I'm sure he will agree."

Surg brought up the subject of medical supplies at the evening discussion, and their idea for Larissa, Krysl, and Rubicor to go to the cave and learn the medicine woman's trade. Millen agreed and called for concurrence. Moka, who was now a regular member of the colony, said she would lead them there and stay with them. Levey agreed to let Krysl go, with plans to leave on the next solar.

Surg took stock of the medications and general health of the group. He took Stretch aside and discussed an even bigger concern with her.

"My sweet Stretch, you probably won't be surprised, at this, but while keeping track of everyone's health, I've found that some of the females in the colony are pregnant."

"Who? Surg."

"Three couples so far, and I'll announced them at the evening meeting. Hector may be surprised, but Cezanne will probably be first. Rubicor can inform Kirsovich that she is on the way, and Thelana can tell Arvidon that her oven is producing more than pottery ... she has one in her own oven."

"That's wonderful, Surg."

"Remember, I have no medications in case a birth does not go smoothly."

"Surg, you will do fine. I guess we'll become as the natives, and have babies like they do. I just hope the complications will be very minimal, and most of the new citizens will arrive smoothly. By the way, have you tested me for pregnancy Surg?"

"Yes Stretch, and so far its been negative. Your chemical hasn't depleted yet. When you're ready, we'll remove it. We've always planned on a few offspring and Terres is as good a place as any to have them."

* * * *

After the evening meal was completed, Surg waved his hand and announced the forthcoming increases of colonists.

"Are you sure?" Thelana asked. "I don't feel pregnant."

"Quite sure. My tests are very positive. The implant under your skin has long ago been exhausted, and you are pregnant. Our longhouse is going to become a nursery, with many little footsteps in the dust."

He announced, with a smile, that Moka was pregnant. "Also, we are going to be privy to the first known interplanetary cross-specie offspring." His eyes had a twinkle as he explained. "Obviously a Terreling ovum is receptive to a Baetian male cell, because Moka is also pregnant. Her baby will be a hybrid, from Caleb. I hope it will be healthy and survive?" he said.

"Barring any catastrophe, this colony is going to build a big nursery in the spring, and our long term perpetuity is going to include a mixing of the species."

Krysl heard him discuss lack of medicines.

"Surg," she said. "We have learned so much about natural herbs from the medicine woman already, that we can make many analgesics. They will have to suffice. Life will go on."

Surg agreed. "I guess we'll be as the natives, and use their medicines. We'll find out soon. For starters, we have an epidemic of respiratory problems in the colony, and Praetor is not responding well to his infection. The comfrey the medicine woman put on him is helping, but not fast enough."

In spite of the booster vaccine the colonists had received from Clodea back on Baeta, some of the party came down with Terres respiratory and muscular ailments. Their immune systems could not ward off every intruder they were exposed to. With fevers and weakness in many, Rami conferred with Clodea for help.

"Rami, the solution I used to preserve the organs, you know, the one that started to dissolve the rubber, is a strong virus inhibitor. If we can salvage some from the batch of chemicals I have, we can give Praetor some internally and see how he responds. I have taken it internally myself, and have not had any side effects except giving the user strong, pungent, sea-shore breath. We'll call it Clodea's secret elixir.

Rami retrieved the container of the di-petryl sulfur compound and gave himself an oral dose. He immediately had a sense of well being and began to feel energetic. He approached Surg with his proposal to give Praetor some, and asked how we might administer it.

"We could inject it, or administer it intravenously," he said. "We need to do something soon, or we'll lose him. Poor fellow has cephalic edema, infection at the compound fracture, and probably some of the viruses that have hit others in our group."

Clodea said it may help, but not as an injection. "I think the stuff is too reactive to inject, but let's start a dilute IV and see if it helps."

"All right," said Surg, "but I wish Krysl were here; she is better at finding veins than I am."

"Let me do it," said Clodea. "Surg, I had to find veins in rodents as part of my research. I'm very good at it."

"Very well. Get your compound and let's try it. We have little to lose."

Within one solar after the IV began, Praetor started to respond favorably. His eyes began to focus, his fever began to subside and he was thirsty. Rami told Clodea to give each person who felt unusual symptoms an oral dose, mixed into a natural tea. Surg asked Rami what he was doing and he said "trying to get ahead of the fevers, before it decimates the entire group."

"I hope it helps, Rami, because I'm getting overwhelmed, and there's not much I can do to help anyone, except administer analgesics, and our supply of those is getting low. I hope we can get more from the medicine woman."

36. CORKY AND CERE

Cere was emotionally drained over Pylar's death. Although their relationship was not close, she was more shocked than anyone over his death, and a loss is traumatic, regardless of the depth, or lack of, in the relationship.

Cere found consolation in loving on the new child in the compound. She would move to spend time playing with Rubel, but to her dismay found other women also wanted to hold and cuddle with the baby. She had to take turns just holding her. Having Rubel in the compound stirred the maternal instincts of many of the colony females, including Cere, and several desired to have a child of their own.

Corky, as commander of Skyflier, was an authority figure for Cere on the flight, and the subliminal attraction continued after they became a colony on the ground. In a way, corky was still an authority figure, and it was natural that in her grief, she looked to Corky for comfort.

Cere had always tried to maintain a cheerful attitude in spite of Pylar's indifference; and it was her nature to be flirtatious. She flirted with all the males, but Corky was her main target most of the time.

Once the colony was established on the ground, this made Corky uncomfortable, because he was sharing a bed with Larissa, and felt a loyalty to her. Also, he didn't want to see another flare of jealousy from Pylar like he saw during the flight. So, he did his best to ignore Cere's flirtations, but secretly his ego soared because she had singled him out.

At Pylar's burial ceremony, she leaned against Corky for support. He put his arms around her and held her tightly for a long time. She felt the vibrations in his body and sensed that he was exchanging empathy as her future soul mate. Corky knew, at that moment, she was eventually going to become his Terres pledgemate. How he would tell Larissa and how she would take it he didn't know, but suddenly he realized he'd had strong feelings for Cere, even way back on the Skyflier voyage. He was too much the gentleman to express his feelings and create a conflict then, or even now in the colony, but he couldn't hold his feelings back forever, living in the same compound as they were. He had to resolve this enigma and settle it, now.

He put his arms around her again, and she returned the intimacy.

Several solars later, he asked Larissa to go for a walk with him, that he had something to tell her.

"I know, Corky. You don't need to say it. I've known for a long time, but I was enjoying our time together, and the physical acts were good. I even kept a rein on my feelings until I thought I was pregnant, but it was a false alarm, and frankly I was disappointed. I wanted a baby. I've talked to Clodea about it and she said not to be concerned, that she brought a large variety of frozen semen with her from Baeta, as a contingency. I'll survive, get pregnant with artificial insemination, and you are free, no obligations, no strings."

"And you are a wonderful person Flower. I wish I had given you the baby you wanted, but Clodea will fix you up."

37. PRAETOR'S POINT

Levey sometimes opened an evening meeting with some *thanks and reflections* on events that had recently taken place.

"The warrior is gone, and Praetor's arm is healing," he said. "We have to accept the fact that Pylar is gone, and take care of each other so illness or accidents don't claim more of us."

The group applauded Levey. Praetor showed everyone how well he was progressing by flexing his arm, and twirling a sling around his head to accent the movement.

Many questions always came Praetor's way, for as an archeologist and a student of ancient civilizations on Baeta, he would make comparisons of native customs here with cultures back home. He was also an interesting speaker. Of particular interest to him were the apparent changes that came with technical advances. The presence of the colonists here on Baeta, he speculated, would change the life styles and habits of the natives forever.

Praetor wanted to make a point of weaponry development.

"First priority of any culture, and ours is no exception, is providing for food and shelter. When those basics are taken care of, new innovations usually come into prominent use only if they ease the burdens or help obtain the basic necessities. Bone needles for example, used by these natives for fastening skins into clothing, made sewing more productive. Weaving has become such a fine art here, almost competitive among these natives, that the skills are incredible. You've all seen their baskets. Some are so tight they can hold water. The weaving will eventually be replaced by pottery. The question of why they haven't already baked clay, or invented slingshots, or bows and arrows is a mystery to me, but apparently they are contented with what they have now."

"We can show them many things to make life easier for them," Rami said.

"A lever is a powerful tool. Pottery and metal craft are certainly big advances. These few things alone will be make their lives so much better."

"Better than what?" Praetor looked around the group. "Does anyone remember what caused the demise of our home planet?" He answered himself. "Technological advances. We advanced ourselves into extinction."

"How so?" Fraya asked. "I don't agree. We knew planet overheating was a problem but we could have stopped it."

"Fraya, why couldn't we return home?" Praetor continued his questions.

"We lost our contact, and communications."

"What caused it to be lost?"

"EMP; burning out communication circuits."

"What caused the EMP?"

145

"Nuclear explosions," she replied.

"And now I can make my point, people. The natives are surviving in their own ways, with their spears, flints, and fire. We have now shown them how to make a bow and arrow. Soon, they will hunt with the bow and arrow at first, but before long it will become an offensive weapon for them. Their ability to make war will rise a notch higher. Their defense will continue to be the spear, but they can turn it into an improved offensive weapons with a slinger that can throw a spear farther and more accurately than before.

"Then there will be a technology plateau, until we make explosive powder and give it to the Terrelings. We'll get some sulfur and nitrate salts, to mix with charcoal and make explosives: We will make hollow tubular rods to fire a steel ball with the explosive powder. Then we'll give the Terrelings some of the tubes and the explosive powder. By then, Terrelings will be a mixture of the natives and our own offspring. Their offense will become barbarian. The tubes and steel balls will be blowing off people's limbs and doing damage to human targets that are over hills and out of sight. These are not scenes from my imagination; these are scenes from history books on our planet.

"We will develop power sources so that our descendants can live a better, more comfortable life. We'll have electrical power for buildings, and finally, Terrelings of the future, a mix of 'us and them' will make explosives that can cause EMP to occur on this planet, as it did on Baeta. The same progression will eventually occur here, until this planet fails to support life, as happened on Baeta."

"You make us sound like criminal intruders, Praetor." Millen said.

"In a way, we are. But things will change whether we interfere or not. Clodea can and has altered dna, so we know it can be done.

146

Nature also alters dna, in her own way and time, making mutants. Some of the mutants survive. Rami says common dna could have grown or evolved in this solar system, but more likely it came from the outside, carried by a comet or asteroids, and sprinkled on all the planets. It was bound to arrive here, and therefore similar dna will eventually be found on all the planets.

"We have an opportunity to leave our knowledge and history for future generations, and hopefully they will take better care of this planet than we did back home. Even if our offspring work toward keeping a better environment, in the long run it won't do any good. Motives are shaped by, *what's in it for me now?* and action usually takes the path of *repair* rather than *prevent*."

38. THE SMELTER AND FORGE

The colony settled in the longhouse before the first snow arrived, and had established a routine for survival from the cold. The supply of light petrol for heating and cooking ran out, as expected and they used wood for fuel. From the clay they made bowls and utensils, which they shared with the tribe. The natives seemed to catch on and learn new technology quickly, and actually began shaping some clay into utensils. However, they preferred to let Thelana cure them in her oven, rather than construct an oven of their own.

The colonists had taught the natives to use flint blades with handles for small axes, and the iron blades for heavier work. The iron axes were very useful and easy to use when it came to breaking up wood for the fires. Arvidon kept busy smelting iron ores and making tools, and as his skill improved, he fashioned new bellows from horsehide, further improving his production. Charcoal was used for heating the forge, and he requested Praetor tend the charcoal factory.

Praetor had responded quickly to Clodea's elixir, and was up and about asking to participate in chores. An assigned activity was good therapy for Praetor, and his stamina returned quickly. He became manager of the charcoal factory.

Surg kept Praetor's broken arm in a splint and temporarily immobilized, so he had to tend the charcoal factory one-handed. His handicap was not a problem, as he had lots of help from Arg's hunters. The charcoal factory consisted of a large, clay vessel over an open fire, in which wood was roasted until it quit gassing. The charcoal vat was then air-cooled and the charcoal dumped out. Then more wood was added, and the process repeated. To speed production, they made a second clay vat so they could alternate from fire to fire, and roast one while the other was cooling.

Most of Arg's hunters were content to gather wood and watch Praetor make charcoal, rather than shape and cure clay themselves. The cooperative effort for the charcoal and smelting went smoothly until one of the hunters got burned. Fire and the heat it generated was not new to the natives, and most had small burn spots from sparks, but this warrior got a severe burn on an arm when a glowing log flipped onto him.

Moana, the medicine woman was nearby and immediately covered the burn with a sticky balm from a herb she freshly plucked. The warrior winced at first, but the soothing action of the herb began to take effect, and ease the pain. The warrior continued helping with the wood gathering.

The natives were especially impressed by the bellows, and the smelting of iron ingots. They wanted to help pump the bellows to heat the forge; however, Praetor had trouble getting them to stop when the forge was hot enough. He had to shout and scold, and finally they understood his signals and stopped at Praetor's signal.

148

The vinewood they used for the bows and arrows had to be cut by shaving the stalk with flint knives, or chopped with the small ax from the colony's bag of tools. The new axes Arvidon produced, helped with wood cutting, but the first ones he forged were heavy and wieldy. He kept getting better with experience.

Eventually, Arvidon made a sword, and deemed it had other uses than for defense. The sword had a wide, curved tip, and could cut brush and vinewood. Rami and Caleb tried it at the vine grove to cut poles, and it worked very nicely. However, the sword was very heavy and hard to maneuver, so Arvidon made some that were thinner and lighter, and sharpened on both sides. In the event of an attack, the wielder of the light sword could easily turn his hand over and backswing, or swing forward either way. Arvidon made several to be ready for defense in case they were attacked again, but hoped they would never be used in battle. Then he saw warriors practicing with the swords, whacking at poles, and knew it was only a matter of time until they used them offensively in battle.

Among other items that Arvidon fashioned were knife blades that could be spliced into a wooden handle with strips of animal hide. When natives saw a knife forged by Arvidon, they asked to have some knives of their own. Arvidon was kept busy forging knife blades, as well as swords and tools.

Moka, Krysl, Larissa and Rubicor, who had gone to learn the natives' way for medicines, arrived back in a few solars, and had brought several of the native women with them. Moka had been a useful interpreter and they learned much from the medicine woman. They even brought back some of the dried herbs she gave them, and started explaining their use to Surg. Some of them were laxatives, some reportedly helped infections and fevers, and some of them were analgesics. One of them made an intoxicating tea like Rami had drunk at the cave and Surg wondered about its usefulness as a medicine.

"An effective tranquilizer, I think, if used in moderation."

The supply given to them was not very large because the medicine woman didn't want to deplete her supplies. Most of the herbs are gathered during the growing season, so Larissa and Liev realized they would have to make many field trips when the weather warmed, learn to recognize the growing plants, and gather their own supplies.

Zema and Moana, the medicine woman, went over to Fraya and examined her. "Baby fine, but has small neck," said Zema. "May not live."

"Neck is fine, Zema," said Fraya. "It is normal. All sky people have small necks." She emphasized the statement by rubbing her neck with her hand. Zema was skeptical but accepted the possibility the baby would live with a small neck, like the other sky people.

Fraya kept Rubel covered with the soft fur blanket Moka had made, and had her standing with help before long. She also recognized that the colonists did not have enough warm clothing for a cold season.

"Maggie," Fraya called, "I think you and Moka should teach the other women to make fur vests similar to what Arg wears."

"Good idea, Fraya. Moka is already thinking of that, and said they needed to hunt and bring back lots of floppy-ears, for the pelts."

So, along with gathering wood and making charcoal; hunting for the floppy-ears became a daily chore.

39. THE COLD SEASON

The deciduous leaves had turned from green to kaleidoscopic red and yellow, with some brown streaks. Water containers would greet the colonists with a flimsy crust of ice that had to be broken for morning access to the liquid below it.

"The leaves are quite beautiful, Rami. Reminds me of home at the end of the long solar period." Fraya held some leaves in one hand, and caressed them with her other hand.

"They are similar, Fraya. Obviously, photosynthesis is the same on both planets."

"I know you are thinking of capillaries and photosynthesis, Rami, but for now, just enjoy the beauty of the leaves."

She wove a garland of leaves and placed it on Rubel's head. Rubel tilted her chin up inviting some nuzzling to her neck, and let out a hearty laugh when she felt Fraya's lips touch her.

"You can see beauty in most everything, Fraya, and I love that in you. It's going to be fascinating to watch some Baetian seeds grow here, and perhaps we can get some fruit trees started, too. We did bring some seeds from fruits, didn't we? Pollination surely must take place here as it does on Baeta."

Wild grasses were brown and ripe. Liev and Larissa gathered many for their farming experiments, and Moka curiously followed them, watching, as they harvested the grains. She had seen Liev cooking some of them in hot water, but now they were doing something she could not understand. They were putting some of the seeds in the ground, in furrows, near the longhouse, and covering them with dirt. Larissa planned a big experimental cultivation project for the colonists. She wanted to see if seeds would germinate in the ground during the cold season, as they did on Baeta. If so, they would become crop farmers.

Rubel chuckled at the first taste of snow. Her fur lined booties, so warm and soft, left little footprints as she paddied around in the strange, cold, whiteness. She usually ran, rather than walked, and whenever she lost her balance and plumped down backward on her seat, she would giggle and laugh out loud, and fluff the snow with her hands. Those who were watching couldn't help but laugh with her. She was doted by most of the colony women, but Moka had made her strongest *big-sister* bond.

Moka, who became Caleb's mate, was pregnant and beginning to show, but several other colony women were farther along. Three of the ladies, Cezanne, Rubicor, and Thelana displayed prominent abdominal bulges, and all three kept physically and mentally busy. Rubicor ventured out for short periods to check on the ore supply, and Thelana worked the kiln for part of each solar. Cezanne, who continued to make active records in the clay tablets, delivered before the other two, and had a memorable reminder of her birthing solar; heavy snow.

The first snowfall in the compound was light, and had arrived in what the colonists assumed was mid-cold season, (four moons after the freezing started). Maggie had made bedrolls for Moana, the name given to the medicine woman, and Zema so they could move into the longhouse. They wanted to stay for several moons and assist with the births. The first snow never totally melted or left, and when Cezanne delivered her son, a heavy storm piled even more snow, knee deep, and muffled the area outside with a thick, white blanket. Cezanne's delivery went smoothly. She and Hector dubbed their newborn boy Frosty, a name that seemed fitting for the occasion. Rubel would now have a playmate in a few moons, when Frosty started walking.

Rubicor and Thelana consecutively gave birth to girls they named Petal and Gem. Larissa birthed next with a boy, and called him Rocky. Larissa had not gotten pregnant with Corky, so Clodea artificially inseminated her with a sample from her sperm cache.

"What do you think, Stretch," Surg asked his mate. "Are you ready for a child?"

"I think so Surg. Having all these babies around has turned on my hormone pumps, and is stimulating my readiness to conceive. Go ahead and remove the implant, and we'll see if I get pregnant. You don't feel too old, do you?"

"No my Stretch. I think I'm ready to be a parent. And it may be an effort, but I'll be able to keep up with a youngster for awhile yet."

Maggie desired a baby but couldn't seen to conceive with Millen. She was cheerful and optimistic, however.

"I may be a little old, Millen, but maybe later on I'll have Clodea inseminate me."

"That would be fine with me, Maggie," he replied. "Old is only relative, and we have lots of time, and lots of help here in the compound."

Liev had not conceived, and Rami was unsympathetic. He was still smarting from her attempted mutiny, so she was not one of his favorite persons. He was civil to her, but had some uncivil thoughts and whispered them to Fraya: "With her sour disposition, Praetor probably can't get very excited about getting her pregnant."

"Now Rami, you of all people know that not all women are mating magnets."

"Yes," he said. "Especially her. Have you seen her flinch whenever one of the Terrelings touch her?"

"I have, but as long as her attitude doesn't disturb the balance in the colony, let's leave it alone. Besides, if she needs counseling, that's what we brought Levey along for."

"You are so smart, Fraya." He put an arm around her and nuzzled her neck. " Want to try for another pregnancy?"

"In time, Rami. Let's let nature take its course here."

The next declarations of pregnancy came soon after, at an evening meeting. Corky and Cere announced that Cere had one on the way. Levey and Krysl said they were expecting, and Clodea announced she had inseminated herself, and it had taken.

"I have sperm samples from many of you males in the colony, as well as some I brought along from Baeta. Thanks, boys. For Larissa I used a sample from a Baetian donor. For myself, I used one from the colony. I am not going to tell anyone whose sample I used, so if appearances are any measure of paternity, you can all wait and be surprised when my baby is born."

40. WARM SEASON BEGINS

The longhouse did become a nursery during the cold months and within a few moons five of the children were walking. Those scampering about were Rubel, Frosty, Petal, Gem, and Rocky, and the parents occasionally let them play outdoors in the snow. Other babies were being born but at this stage, they were infants and not yet walking. The hunting and smithing were curtailed and colony activities were mostly limited to fire tending and cooking.

"How many moons before the weather begins to warm, Moka?" Millen asked.

Moka discussed the question with her mother and other tribal people, and finally held up three fingers: "Three more moons. We go through this each time the snow season comes, and then it gets warm again, and the snow melts."

"It is a good thing we made a storehouse and put away food supplies," Rami said to Millen. "We were guessing about how long or severe the cold season would be, but apparently our guess was fairly accurate."

Fraya knew the orbital cycles of all the planets, and clarified for Rami and Millen.

The only reason to go outside in the snow was to replenish the wood pile in the longhouse or bring in food supplies from the storehouse, and most of the colonists worked together to accomplish these chores. Some of the intelligencers of the colonists had batteries that still worked, so reading was a valuable pastime. Some games were invented such as casting a ball from one side of the longhouse to the other, but boredom was a dangerous side effect of confinement.

"Rami," Fraya said, "the noisy children and confinement are making me frustrated. You know what I miss? Music.

"Can you make me a flute, Rami? I can't play, but some of the people or the children will have musical talent and will learn, I am sure."

Rami found something besides cooking and farming that interested Liev. Before she was recruited on Baeta, Liev was a musician and teacher.   When Rami mentioned making some instruments, her attitude brightened and she coached Rami and Praetor on making several musical instruments. She helped design them, and even helped make them. From vinewood, they made flutes of different lengths and hole patterns. Drums were fashioned from hide and hollowed logs. Strings were made from thin strips of hide and dried floppy-ear innards, and stretched across wooden acoustical boxes.

Most of the colonists had some talent or interest in music and took up the instruments. Before long, a flood of diaphanous sounds echoed around the longhouse. The natives were curious about the instruments and the sounds, but slow to use them. They generally seemed to lack rhythm or talent.

"I believe the lack of acceptance is because they don't see any point to it," Praetor said. "It's not hunting, fighting, or gathering, those activities that matter to them, so why do it?"

"Maybe so, but rhythm is intuitive to the nervous system," said Liev, "and I predict we'll see many of them drumming and dancing to a cadence before long."

She was right. Some of the hunters watched and mimicked others pounding on a drum and could hardly stay still. Native feet were soon moving up and down with the beat and then dancing with an alternating slapping of feet on the floor.

As the lights got longer and the snow began to melt, several new babies were born to the colonists in a second wave of births. There were three new mothers; Cere, Krysl and Clodea. To listen to Corky boast, one would think he had done the actual birthing himself, instead of Cere, but he proudly showed everyone the son he and Cere produced. Krysl gave Levey a boy, and they seemed pleased to be in the parent circle, giving Zhu most of the credit. Clodea artificially inseminated herself, with a colonist donor and said she would not tell who the donor was. She assumed there would be a paternity resemblance, but when there wasn't, she confessed to using Kel's sperm. "We've been sharing a bed most of the time anyway, so I don't really know if the conception was natural or artificial, but either way, it is Kel's."

"Thank you, Clodea, she is beautiful," Kel said. "I will have so much fun with her. If I can build a big, controllable kite that I can launch off a ledge, I'll teach her to fly."

"I'll fly it too, " Corky said. "We'll have some fun, and maybe some time we could even build an engine, and make a stratocraft."

* * * *

156

There were three other women who were pregnant but trailed the others in incubation time by a few moons . Surg announced, at the evening meeting, that Stretch was pregnant, and the group gave them an ovation. Maggie had finally conceived, and the group wished her and Millen well. Of particular interest to Surg was Moka who had gotten pregnant by Caleb. Surg could hardly contain himself. He was interested in how the first cross-specie baby would appear and fare.

Not only were the colony women fertile, but the ground was fertile and producing new growth. Before the last three babies were born, the seeds Liev and Larissa had planted before the snows, began sprouting. Green shoots were poking up from grains, bulbs, and tubers. The colonists were now farmers.

There were cheers and celebrations by the colonists, celebrating the new growth, and it was infectious. The five older children joined in the cheers with dancing and hand clapping, and Fraya felt like they understood what was happening by their actions. Whether they did or not didn't matter; the cheerful attitude swept through the colonists and they were happy about it.

Rami had spotted a herd of the small curlyhorns near their field that were calving and got as close as he dared to watch the process. The snow was mostly gone, but the ground was cold and slushy. The nearest female dropped a newborn onto the damp ground. He watched it pop up onto its feet and stagger around until it got its bearings as the female licked and cleaned the steaming calf. She stood still while it nuzzled for a teat. Rami knew something about animal husbandry from his biology background on Baeta, and guessed that this was a seasonal event all over their area, possibly for horse, ox, and bighorns as well as curlyhorns.

A snarling growl caught his attention as a canine dashed up to the female and attacked the calf, tearing at a leg. The female curlyhorn attempted to ward off the canine, but it was too agile and dodged aside. The canine crouched and sprung again at the calf, now bawling and confused. Rami pulled out his sling and hit the canine with a rock, knocking it unconscious. By then he was joined by Corky, Kel, and Caleb, who had been watching from the edge of the field. Rami instructed the three pilots to bind the canine and catch the limping calf, and bring them to the compound. The female curlyhorn stood nearby, bleating in a state of bewilderment, and Kel said he might also be able to catch her too. The female was only about half the size of a man. Kel took a length of horsehide rope, threw it over the head and horns of the female, and wrestled her to the ground. A second rope was slung around her neck and Corky held that one. While Caleb carried the calf in his arms, the female with Corky and Kel on each side seemed willing to follow Caleb and the calf to the compound without a struggle. She was almost docile in her submission to the ropes held by Corky and Kel.

"Where did you learn to handle animals like that, Kel?" Rami asked.

"I grew up on a grassland and had lots of animals to tend," Kel replied.

"Now what are we going to do with these animals, Rami?" Corky had withdrawn a knife and was preparing to butcher the curlyhorns. He assumed that was what Rami had in mind.

"No corky, we are not going to kill them. First, let's see if we can tame them. We need milk for the children and we can get some milk from the female. Perhaps we can entice more curlyhorns to get close enough to capture, and if we do, maybe we can develop a herd. I just feel they can be domesticated and if so we can use them for meat, milk, and fleece. If it doesn't work, we can butcher them later."

"The female was sure easy to catch," Kel said. "And obviously she wanted to be with the calf. At home, we take hair like hers and comb it into fibers, then spin it into threads. The threads can be woven into cloth. I believe we could do that with these animals."

"What about this canine," asked Corky. "He had killing on his mind."

"That's true, he did," Rami said, "but he wasn't doing anything evil. He was just hungry and trying to make a living the only way he knows how. Also, if you'll look closer, it isn't a *he;* it happens to be a female ready to deliver pups. She is full of milk, lactating, and ready to give birth. I think it is time we consider having some pets in the compound, so let's see if we can tame her, and train some of her pups."

41. THE COLONY AND HERDS GROW

The curlyhorn calf and female were hand fed, and easily tamed as a result of being tethered and fed at regular times. Milking the female at first required two men to hold her while Kel did the milking. He had spent his childhood on a grassland on Baeta, and learned to tend animals and milk them when he was growing up. He was enjoying the role of herdsman, and sometimes wondered how he got sidetracked into becoming a pilot, but had no regrets. Herding animals was a different form of fun, but Corky was glad Kel became a pilot. Kel, as a co-pilot, had helped Corky several times get out of extreme hazardous situations.

The canine was also tethered, and thrived, seemingly happy to be getting regular meals without the strain of hunting for food. Her growling discouraged anyone from hand feeding her, but she readily gobbled the meat that was thrown into her pen. Rami, with help, built her a small shelter where she delivered her pups and took care of them. They kept her tethered in the pen but before long the pups would wander out of the pen and investigate the children. They would sniff and nuzzle, with trepidation but not with fear. She had six pups to nurse and take of, and some of the braver pups began frolicking and running with the children. The pups became a new bond in the pack, and at sleep times most of the six pups could be seen in the pile of children. Although the pups became friendly with the humans, the female reminded those around her that she was still a wild animal and never fully acceptable to the tether, or the closeness of humans.

* * * *

Moka got through a strained delivery. The cross-baby was a boy and it appeared not much different from the Baetian babies, except stockier and the neck was shorter. He appeared strong and bright. Caleb suggested Terba as a name, to combine Terreling and Baetian, and Moka was agreeable to that name. Zema helped with the birth and was obviously proud of her new grandson, but a little apprehensive about his mixed parentage. She wondered if Terba would live, and if so, would he be accepted by other tribal children. That worry was short-lived, because the colony children and the tribal children were already living and playing together. The five older children mostly slept in a pile of furs in the middle of the floor, with arms and legs poking out in all directions. This was the way of pack animals, but now they were joined by tribal children, and the pups.

After the snow was mostly gone, the colony was once again frequently visited by Arg's people and new children from the tribe joined in the activities and games. They got along well, and at sleep time, the tribal children joined the pile of arms, legs, and bodies in the pile on the floor.

"We seem to be pack animals regardless of our heritage," Levey commented. "That pile of children certainly looks like a contented pack."

"What do you mean by *pack,?* Krysl asked Levey as she patted her abdomen.

"It means we prefer being in the company of others, instead of by ourselves, Krysl."

"Then ours will be joining the Pack shortly, Levey. I am so glad we were accepted into the colony and came on this trip. The environment back home was deteriorating very rapidly, and I think this will be a good place for our child to grow."

"I totally agree, Krysl. We will be in the history books that Cezanne is writing, the history of a colony on Terres."

42. THE CHILDREN MAKE AN IMPACT

The light period was a time of happiness for Fraya. On Baeta, she never did like the dark except for star gazing. Her interest in the stars and planets never waned, and before Rubel was born, she again turned her attention to the night sky. She had a pair of magnivisors and frequently stared upward. Besides the sporadic quick flash of a meteorite hitting the atmosphere she occasionally saw the glow of Alpha-Surf, that first Baetian orbiter Lockni sent to circle Terres. It was still orbiting and sometimes would appear as a star streaking across the sky. Before the mad Glennick caused Barge to crash, she could frequently see its bright reflection.

After Rubel was born, she would sit with the baby on her lap wrapped in robes and watch the stars. The nights were peaceful and quiet except for the wind, and occasional animal calls. Baeta has no moon so moon watching on Terres was especially inspirational and delightful to her. She knew its cycle by memory and studied it mainly for its beauty. When the sky was clear, the moon's craters were discernible through the magnivisors, and she could see shadows down inside some of them.

There were various strange sounds in the night, and Fraya learned to recognize many of them. Most were caused by the wind bending trees or rolling a loose bush, but others were animal noises. One sound she heard frequently was hooting in a staccato pattern, but she never saw what made it.

She was sometimes frightened by the howling during the night. *Canines probably*, she imagined, *like we had back on Baeta*. The animals that howled seldom seemed to show themselves, but obviously stayed in packs and were communicative during the dark. It seemed to her sometimes a whole pack would be howling all at the same time, and the harmony was terrible. Other packs would answer. Fraya sometimes thought the animals might be objecting to the intruding skypeople. She also had thoughts they might be organized and having community meetings, with elections, and campaigns; and then she would laugh, mostly to Rubel, as she imagined one canine sitting on its haunches, chairing a meeting.

Some of the noises made the hair on the back of her neck stiffen, and reminded her of the groaning structure in the spaceship when they were fueling and waiting for launch. She worried the animals might try to raid their larder and be aggressive if encountering a colonist, but Rami tried to reason that animal conduct was probably predictable, in that they would not attack a human unless cornered or defending some territory.

Rubel and the older children began walking before the spring arrived, and frequently played outside with the animals. The pups and the curlyhorns became tame, but the female canine continued to growl at anyone who got close. Rami decided to release her to the wild, so she could find a mate and have more puppies. She would disappear at night, but would return during the solar, go into the pen on her own, and give the puppies some attention. She would lick their faces and clean them. Some would still try to nurse.

The first five, Rubel, Frosty, Petal, Gem, and Rocky were actively running around and forming vocabularies of their own. They were communicating with each other to the amazement of Maggie. The language of the five included gestures and many new words from the natives that Maggie didn't fully understand, but Fraya assured her it was not a concern.

"Don't worry Maggie, they know what they're saying."

The children, tribal and colonist, understood each other and could make the adults understand when they needed to. Fraya called it *babblespeak*. One child would make up a new word at will, and the others would pick it up and use it like it had always been around.

The older five were followed by the curlyhorns and the puppies when they were outside and Fraya could see that an irreversible integration of Terrelings, Colonists, and animals was taking place for the better. Survival was still their main objective, now that Barge and Skyflier had crashed, the integration was their hope for sharing lifestyle and survival.

Terba, a little younger than the others, was mischievous, and liked to wander from the compound. Moka would scold him and restrict him, but his interest lay outside the colony. He loved and fondled the animals. When the puppies followed him, he would play *fetch*, with a ball of hide, and *tug of war* with a leather thong. Some of the other

163

children copied him and joined in the play, but Terba had the strongest natural bonding of all the children with the animals.

Kel and Caleb became the animal tamers for the colonists and Caleb was proud to have his son work with him. Terba was too young to start milking the female curlyhorn, but he would try and he actually understood the process. Kel and Rami had found several other calving curlyhorns, and with Caleb's help captured them. As a result, during the first year the colonists developed a large herd of curlyhorns and from their milk began making cheese and cream products. They combed their coats and got long fibers from the fur and hair. Enthusiasm grew about spinning the long fibers into threads. Many of the tribal women were excellent basket weavers and quickly learned to use the animal threads for weaving curly hair fibers into cloth. Some of the colonists became proficient at dying the threads, so weaving colorful patterns into cloth became an art. Most of the children also showed an interest in weaving and the craft evolved into a major community activity.

The children, both boys and girls, participated in community chores. Beside cooking and fire tending, they herded the curlies from pasture to pasture in the summer. By the second year, Terba had started climbing onto the back of some of the young curlies and riding them. Mostly they would buck and kick their back legs into the air, and the youngster would fall off. Not to be deterred, Terba would climb back on and ride again. Rubel tried riding a curly and screamed with delight at the thrill of the activity. Her balance was not as good as Terba's, so she would promptly bounce off, with more screaming and laughter. She and Terba became inseparable companions, and spent most of their waking time with the animals.

Maggie finally conceived without Clodea's artificial help. She was the last of the colony women (except Liev who didn't seem to care) to get pregnant. Maggie looked over the flock of youngsters and realized they may have to eventually build a bigger longhouse when more babies arrived. Also, some of the natives seemed to have moved their children into the longhouse and the mix of children sometimes got confusing.

43. THE COLONISTS BECOME FARMERS

As the weather warmed and the solar periods got longer, seeds that sprouted before the snow came, began to host new growth. When it was cold, most of the young, green sprouts had turned brown and looked dead, but new shoots were now making an appearance next to the brown dead shoots. Moka and the other natives were so impressed with the neat rows of sprouting plants and the process of cultivation , some wondered out loud why they hadn't tried it before. Planting had actually been done many times by the natives, by accidentally dropping seeds, but no one apparently made a connection between new growth and dropping seeds.

The new sprouts grew into stalks or vines, and the grains formed heads laden with seeds. By the time the weather became hot and the sun appeared to stay light more than half the time, fiber cores covered with yellow kernels were forming, and the heads of grain were turning a tan color. Vines snaking around the yard grew fleshy, long fruits that could be baked or boiled.   Other fleshy plants were multicolored spheres, and had flavor and texture similar to the longer, tubular plants. The pungent bulbs dug from the wild patches of growth were separated into seedling pieces and planted. The seedlings pushed through the earth exposing their tops, and multiplied to provide a bounty of piquant seasonings for the cooks.

Liev and Larissa harvested several baskets of golden tan grains, and saved about half for planting before next cold season. The harvest of seeds, fruits, and bulbs provided a flavorful diet for the mixture of colonist and native residents. Agriculture became a practical way of life for the colonists and the Terrelings, and the compound began to look like a farming community, with animals roaming about and gardens adorning the area around the longhouse. More and more vegetables were being grown, and many of the tree seeds that were brought from Baeta and planted had sprouted. Although the trees were small and young, some blossomed by the second annum and were bearing a few small fruits.

During the next several annums, the colonists expanded the herd of curlies to more than twenty females that provided ample milk and meat. Almost all of the curlies gave birth, and some even had twins.

The children took turns herding the curlies from pasture to pasture, and several learned how to milk the lactating females. Curly-herding became part of the duties of the children.

Weaving curly fibers into cloth became a major tribal craft, and many happily wore vests and shoulder covers of woven cloth as a substitute for the heavy animal skins they usually wore. Some of the colonists became proficient at dying the threads, and weaving colorful patterns into the cloth. Pattern weaving became a specialized craft. Some of the women developed symbols with their craft and wove the patterns into their products. Now the men and children could distinguish themselves by wearing a robe or tunic with a specific symbol woven into it.

Rubel, at a very young age, showed an artistic talent that was the envy of many colony women. Rather than weave a pattern into cloth, which she could do with ease, she would weave plain cloth with no colored thread patterns and then paint animal scenes and patterns on the cloth, with her dyes and pigments. Her animal patterns were so graceful and beautiful, Fraya urged her to paint some of them on the walls of Arg's cave. Moka took her to the cave and held bowls of burning tallow for light as she painted. Terba followed Rubel around as usual, and even tried to produce some paintings, but he did not possess the natural talent that Rubel had.

Stretch, Surg's mate was a physical therapist that kept tracking the bodily health of the colonists. When she found that most stayed in good condition from normal chore activity, she decided to become a medical team member with Surg and Krysl, and try to learn the natural remedies of the natives. She spent time with Moana and became proficient at identifying the herbs and plants she used, and their applications. As such, she became an able helper for Surg and Krysl.

Surg, Stretch, and Krysl absorbed much wisdom from the medicine woman, and under her guidance harvested herbs and plants that were beneficial to healthcare. Moana was a patient teacher and her knowledge of natural homeopathy seemed to be instinctive, lore handed down through generations of care-givers. Moka had some of the instinct, especially about the herbs and plants. All three people on the colony medical team recognized they, too, had some instinct for natural healing, albeit not as highly developed as the medicine woman, but enough that Surg thought the instinct could be nurtured and raised to a higher level with practice and usage. *Perhaps all of us have some innate consciousness about our well being,* he thought, *but gets lost from disuse. The ability for care is certainly evident among animals who tend each other and themselves when wounded. We should learn from their behavior when it comes to preservation.*

44. THE CROSSBOW

Arg had seen some of Wigor's tribesmen hunting with bow and arrow, and when he talked to them about it, was told they made them like the one they took from the Sky creature in the vinewoods. Arg knew they had stolen the concept from Pylar when they attacked and killed him and Praetor predicted Wigor's warriors would mimic Pylar and make their own. They had seen Pylar pull the bowstring and shoot arrows at them. After the battle they had taken Pylar's bow and arrows, figured out how to use them, and made more. Now they were hunting with the weapons they made, and some were getting very skillful.

This worried Arg because they had no defense against the arrow. For hunting or battle, their spears were aerodynamic wonders, but they could avoid a spear thrown from a distance by leaping out of the way. But the arrow propelled by a bow was much faster, would go farther and more accurately than a spear. Praetor said it is only a matter of time before Wigor or others like him used bow and arrow as an offensive weapon. He urged the colonists to build a defensive or retaliatory weapon, and suggested a crossbow.

Rami had taught many of the colonist to be proficient with the slingshot, and a stone rivaled the bow and arrow in distance and accuracy, but did not have the penetrating power of an arrow.

"Although I predicted weapon development will continually progress until we eventually have the holocaust nuclear weapon here as we did on Baeta, but for now we have to defend ourselves against Wigor and others like him. They have the bow and arrow, so I propose we design and build a crossbow. It will perform like the bow and arrow but will be more powerful, and have a greater range than a hand-held bow, and it might keep aggressors farther away during an attack."

Praetor was not an engineer but he learned the concept from Pylar in discussions, before he was killed. Praetor and Arvidon concocted a device that could fling an arrow farther and more accurately than any hand-held bow. They experimented with various sizes and configurations, but a vinewood bow horizontally fastened to a frame proved excellent. The bow was cocked by forcing the bowstring back with a forked lever until hooked and restrained over a releasable trigger. The lever was removed after the string was hooked and an arrow or spear was loaded on top the bow ready to be fired.

The colony hadn't been attacked since Pylar's death, but they felt ready to defend themselves. Meanwhile, the crossbow was effective in downing a large animal with an arrow instead of driving it over a cliff. The colonists built several, and now had a hunting arsenal of slingshots, spears, hand-held bows, and cross-bows. With these weapons, hunting for wild meat was no longer a difficult task.

The tamed curlyhorns were producing milk from which the colonists produced cream products, and they slaughtered what they needed for meat when necessary, but hunting, especially for many of the less agile curlyhorn cousins was relatively easy. The most illusive of the prey were the horses that were fast and skittish.

45. THE HORSEMAN

Terba loved the beauty and grace of the horses. Even though they were plentiful in the area he felt sympathy for them when they were hunted for meat. Now that the colonists had the curlyhorn for meat, hides, and fibers, he didn't think it was necessary to kill so many horses. Horse hide was still a major leather source but tunics and robes were now being woven from curlyhorn fibers, and many people chose to wear the lighter woven fibers in favor of leather tunics.

Terba, with some help, had captured some young colts and kept them in a corral near the longhouse. He tamed two of them to tether, and would rub their backs and stroke them so they could get the feel of a burden. Caleb, his father, helped him by tying bundles of hide over the backs of the colts to help them feel a load. Terba was getting too big to ride the curlyhorn calves and planned to start riding the colts when they were two annums old. He had a natural, easy bonding way with all the animals and when he entered the corral, the two colts he was training would run to him and push at each other to be the first to get attention from him. Rubel worked with Terba to establish a bonding with the colts, and found that if one was being stroked by Terba, the other would run to her for attention. In time, the brown and white colt adopted her, and the other, all-brown with white feet, adopted Terba.

When the colts were two annums old, Terba wanted to try riding one, and asked his father to help him. Caleb held the tether and Rubel talked in a cooing voice to the animal while stroking his neck. Terba got to the colt's side, and leaped up to drape his body over the horse's back. The colt tried to rear up, but Caleb held the tether and kept him level. He walked around with the horse beside him, and Terba draped over its back. Terba finally swung his leg over the horse's back and moved to an upright position, with legs astride. The straddling technique worked, and they practiced for several solars until the colt was comfortable with the load on its back. They repeated the process with Rubel and her horse, and before long the two of them were circling the corral side by side on the horses. They learned to control the horses with the tether, and eventually left the corral for exploring the hills around the compound from horseback. Rubel

170

enjoyed traveling longer and longer distances on horseback, and together they found several new caves to explore. Rubel left her mark on several with paintings of animals and cave dwellers.

Even though they were very young, when Rubel and Terba reached puberty, they agreed to be pledgemates and occupied a private section of the longhouse together. They had always been close companions since they started walking, and were the leaders of the longhouse children. Rami and Fraya did not interfere with their cohabitation, and knew most of the children would soon begin having children of their own, and the colony would expand. The original adults became grandparents, and with Clodea's help at insemination, a culture of cross-babies was appearing at the cave from native women. The tribal women finally accepted the fact that a long neck was not a detriment to survival of an infant.

Rami and Fraya aged gracefully, staying near the compound and watching the children play and tend chores. Fraya's hair gradually turned silvery gray, as did Rami's. He would sit by her back and brush her hair while they watched the activities. The canines in the compound were plentiful now, and many bonded as pets. The children's play always included some games with the canines.

Rami had long chats with Dominie Roch about spirituality and the families back on Baeta, and Fraya would usually join the conversation. Fraya barely knew Feydor and Raychek, Rami's best friends who lost their daughter Rubel to a respiratory problem.

"If you remember, Levey, you suggested during the eulogy that maybe Rubel's spirit was living somewhere else in the celestrium. If I had a picture of that Rubel, I would show you a strong resemblance to our Rubel here. Our Rubel has a personality and spirit much like the one we lost in Lignus. I'm going to call them Rubel-one and Rubel-two

171

for discussion purposes. Because they are similar in my memories, I could easily believe in some sort of spiritual reincarnation."

"I don't know what to say about that, Rami. When it comes to spirituality, I think each of us can perceive an afterlife in any way that feels comfortable. If your Rubel-two resembles your memories of Rubel-one in Lignus, so be it. I would say it will be best if you don't dwell so much on the past that you elevate your Rubel-one to some pedestal that makes Rubel-two feel inferior. Rubel-one is mostly now an idol in your imagination. Rubel-two is here now and needs your full support."

"That was very well said, Levey. Thank you. I was leaning toward making Rubel-one an idol and I didn't realize it. Rubel-two will get my total support."

Rami spent many solars after that watching Rubel ride her spotted horse around the compound. She was very athletic and independent, and did not want her father's help getting on or off the horse. He encouraged her to paint more and more, and to teach others in the colony the technique.

Rubel became pregnant and gave birth to a boy. Rami was very proud when they named him Ramitoo, a name similar to his, although Fraya wanted him named Ramizia. This was the first second generation child in the compound, and he had more of Rubel's features than Terba's. Terba, even though a mix of Caleb and Moka, had the tribal features of short neck and sloping forehead, and his hair was red as flame. Many cavemen had flame-colored hair. Rubel's hair was straw colored. She had sky-colored eyes like Rami, and her forehead was high and straight. Ramitoo resembled Rubel.

Fraya was ecstatic about becoming a grandmother, and doted on the child as did Rubel. Rubel curtailed her riding for a few moons, but before long was back on her painted horse with Ramitoo sitting on the horse's back in front of her.

By the time he learned to walk, Ramitoo was at ease on the paint's back, and Terba had him riding on the backs of curlyhorns as he did at that age.

The annums passed quickly and Ramitoo learned to handle animals like his father, Terba. He also learned to tend curlies and rode horses with the older children. Ramitoo had an aptitude for many interests and was a busy child. He played music and worked with the animals. He studied some of the parchment writings that Cezanne had collected and put together as a history of the colony. He learned about the stars and planets from Fraya, and wanted to do some documents on his own. He learned about the pottery and metal work, and was fascinated with the landing craft that sat near the compound.

Rubel expressed some restlessness with the routines of the compound. She could cook as well as anyone, weave patterns and color tapestries, and was an excellent artist. She had a versatile interest in the animals, but wanted to explore other areas. She discussed her travel ideas with her mother, and said she would like to take some long exploration trips with Terba.

"Where would you go, and what would you do ?"

"I would like to see the big blue sea I've heard about, and find more caves to paint in. I think I can leave a legacy of our story for others who may find the caves. At least they will see what some of the animals and cave people look like, from the paintings."

"I see." Fraya replied. "Well, you come by it honestly. When I was your age I wanted to travel to a different planet, and am so glad I did. I think you should explore while you can."

"If I do that, I would like to leave Ramitoo with you until we get back. He loves you so and learns so much from you. Would you be acceptable to that?"

"Of course I would. I'll discuss this with your father, but I don't think he would mind taking care of Ramitoo. This may be a good opportunity for you and Terba to learn more about the land that we now live in; knowledge that you can pass on to Ramitoo and the other children when you get back."

46. THE SEPARATION

"Do you ever miss home, Rami."

"This is home, Fraya, and I've never regretted the life we've chosen and lived. The one thing I wonder about is what happened on Baeta? Did life survive and what is it like."

"I don't think we will ever know, Rami, at least in this lifetime. A more relevant question is how will our lives progress on this planet?

"Rami, I'm sure you realize we've been confined to a small area here, limited by our ability to walk."

"I think about it all the time, Fraya. Rubel and Terba have changed that limitation by taming some horses. They can ride ten times as far as one can walk in the same length of time, and have done so. For the colony, transportation will change in time. All us adults in the colony grew up on Baeta riding in mocs and stratocraft, and have the experience of the space trip in our memories. Back home beasts of burden to many of us were a luxury for pleasure, not transportation. Our children will only know transportation by walking or riding on animals that we tame."

Fraya rocked Ramitoo on her lap. As big as he was, he still liked to he held and cuddled. She spoke to Rami but made it sound like

174

she was talking to the child. "The children and now the grandchildren may never see a machine as a mode of transportation, but animals will carry them and pull their carriages for a long time. We can help them by making wheels and showing them how to use them, but I don't see us making an engine in the near future."

"I don't either, Fraya. We would have to figure out how to machine a piston and cylinder, and that technology is a long way off. Meanwhile, we can continue to concentrate on surviving and so far have done pretty well."

"I wish we had means to explore a larger area, Rami. We know of many features around us from images taken by the Alpha-Surveyor satellite, and Corky saw many of them when he was maneuvering to land, but then we were stranded. I made hand sketches of our area from intelligencer images before their batteries exhausted, so we have rough maps, but we'll never actually see much of the surrounding area. However, Rubel and Terba will."

"What do you mean, they will see the area. They already have explored the limits of daylight travel on their horses."

"Rubel and Terba want to take a much longer trip, Rami. She wants to travel along the upper shore of the big blue sea, the one that separates the two continents. She wants to paint pictures of animals and people on the cave walls for others to see, and teach the art of painting to other tribes that they meet. She has the wanderlust and urge to travel and explore like I did, and I can't fault her for that."

"What about Ramitoo? Will she take him along?"

"She wants to leave him with us, until they get back."

"How does Ramitoo feel about that?"

"I don't know. He has not been concerned when they have taken small, overnight trips. He will have to accept it."

"I certainly am willing. Ramitoo will not be lonesome with so many other children around and the curlies and canines. And us, of course. Let's let them go."

47. SUNSET

Ramitoo didn't want his time with playmates interrupted when Rubel and Terba were ready to leave for their trip, but he did run over to Rubel and give her a hug. Then he waved and ran back to his friends. Terba and Rubel had packed a large stock of rations and skins and loaded them onto a pack-horse. Rubel said a tearful good-bye to Rami and Fraya, mounted her paint, and with Terba, rode out of the compound. With the rising sun on their backs, they disappeared from sight over hills to the west. It was several solars before Ramitoo began to miss his mother and Fraya spent extra time with him, joining in his chores and talking about their past. Both Rami and Fraya had some lines of aging weathered into their faces and grey was dominating the color in their hair. Rami chased after Ramitoo and the curlies as they ran out to the pastures, but he found his aging legs wouldn't keep up. He tried to match the pace of Ramitoo but his breath was short, and he would frequently stop and rest. When Rami chased after the child, Ramitoo would leap and laugh with no thought his grandfather might not be able to keep up. One morning, as Rami followed the menagerie of curlies and canines, he fell gasping for breath. Ramitoo dropped next to him and put his arm over Rami's chest.

"Grandfather, what is the matter?"

"I don't know Rati, but my chest hurts and my arm is numb. I think you better get Grandma."

"You stay here and rest, Grandfather. I'll get Grandmother!"

176

He knew something was seriously wrong as he ran back to the longhouse crying. He told Fraya what had happened and she immediately got Millen, Corky, and two other men to go where Rami lay on the ground. They carried him back to the longhouse and put him in his bedroll.

"Rami you old fool, how dare you run and try to keep up with a child that active. Now I'm getting Surg to look after you, and I am going to let you rest now."

"Thank you Fraya. In case I haven't told you lately I've always been crazy about you."

"Oh shush, before I trade you in on a young warrior."

* * * *

In spite of herbal remedies from the medicine woman and vigilance by Surg, Rami never got up again. When he expired, all the colonists and most of Arg's tribe gathered for a burial ceremony that was tradition for the cavemen. Moka led the wailing and Dominie Roch presented an in-depth eulogy. Other than Pylar, Rami was the first of the original colonists to die, and his legacy, voiced by the Dominary, was clear. Rami had befriended the cavemen who helped the colonists survive. The colony was established, shelters were built, technology was already advancing, and the cross-mixing of cavemen and colonists was taking place. The population was expanding.

* * * *

Not many had the artistic skill of Rubel but those who did learned some of the arts from her. Ramitoo, Rubel's son inherited a quick, technical mind from his grandmother, but lacking in artistic skills, decided to create some art in another way. He saw that the metal plates on the space ships were still bright and shiny after years in the elements and asked if he could remove some of them, cut them up, and use them for tablets. Corky agreed and helped with the removal and cutting, a process that took a long time with only the hand tools they had available. They weren't in a hurry. The scribings they put on the metal plates were a combined effort of grandmother, mother, and child. Rubel and her son would sit by Fraya and listen to her, fascinated, as they heard her tell about the stars, and the other planet, and how the colonists got here. Ramitoo scribed star patterns on the plates as coached by Fraya and made a cone-of-precession for the polar stars. He drew the solar-system showing proximity of the two planets, numbers three and four. He drew spaceship outlines and made one plate writing the alphabet and numbers used by the colonists. While the stories were unfolding, points of interest were inscribed onto the plates by the boy. The artwork wasn't colorful like his mother's paintings but she encouraged him, and helped him saying his work was really beautiful. When the plates were finished, the boy showed them to Fraya.

"Where will we put them, grandmother?"

"We'll find a nice cave, and store them in a protected place. Then, we'll just leave them. Someone will eventually find them, and thank us for sharing our stories with them. Won't that be nice, Ramizia?"

"Yes, grandmother."

THE END

ABOUT THE AUTHOR

Dewey Erlwein is a graduate chemical engineer from the University of Utah. As an expert in materials science, he spent a good portion of his career in design of jet aircraft, missiles, and space projects, including the International Space Station. Among his interests and hobbies, he flies small airplanes and is a flight instructor. He believes the current global warming trend is man-made and is a serious concern.

Most of Dewey's writing has been technical, in the form of manuals, specifications, test reports, and technical journals, but here he shows his talent at science fiction. His first novel is *Skytribe*, combining scenarios of space flight and evolution of modern man on Earth. *Skytribe* was released in 2004. This latest novel, *The Colony and the Cavemen* follows the storyline established in Skytribe, and carries the lives of the main characters forward.

The Colony and the Cavemen is a sequel to *Skytribe*.

Printed in the United States
70632LV00003B/169-303